George Martin

Marguerite

Or, the isle of demons and other poems

George Martin

Marguerite
Or, the isle of demons and other poems

ISBN/EAN: 9783337412845

Printed in Europe, USA, Canada, Australia, Japan

Cover: Foto ©Andreas Hilbeck / pixelio.de

More available books at **www.hansebooks.com**

MARGUERITE;

OR, THE ISLE OF DEMONS

AND OTHER POEMS

BY

GEORGE MARTIN.

MONTREAL:
DAWSON BROTHERS, PUBLISHERS.
1887.

GAZETTE PRINT, MONTREAL.

GEORGE MARTIN'S

POEMS.

A

CONTENTS.

C

X.   CONTENTS.

CONTENTS.

MARGUERITE.

PREFATORY NOTE.

The story narrated in the following poem is one of the most touching of the many romantic legends of the early history of Canada. Some foundation in fact it undoubtedly has, for it forms the basis of one of the stories in the collection of Queen Margaret of Navarre, written while the chief actors in the tragedy were alive. The version of Queen Margaret differs from that of Thevet in many respects. He gives for his authorities Roberval and the unfortunate Marguerite herself.

Parkman, in the first volume of his admirable series of histories—the Pioneers of New France—gives the story as related by Thevet. The subject readily lends itself to poetical treatment, and, if the heroine in the poem is made to put a more favourable construction upon her conduct than the chronicler, it is surely no more than, as the narrator of her own story, she might have a right to do. The harsh and tyrannical character of Roberval is drawn in dark lines by Parkman. His cruelties, in the short lived colony at Cap Rouge, were such than even the Indians were moved to pity

for his victims. On his return to France he was
assassinated at night in the streets of Paris, probably
by the hand of one who had suffered from his tyranny.

In these prosaic days of ocean steamers, cable
telegraphs and light-houses, it is difficult to realize
the mystery which, in old days, enshrouded the shores
of the Western continent. The imaginations of the
daring sailors who in their little vessels explored the
stormy seas of the West, teemed with stories of
dangers, spiritual as well as physical. In those days
of supernaturalism, Satan might well stand guard
over the great world, where, until then, he had held
undivided sway. This Isle of Demons was one of
his outposts. On Wytfliet's Map (1597), *I. de las
Demonios* is laid down to the North of Newfoundland,
but too far out of Roberval's course to be the island of
our story. It is necessary to the narrative that the
island in question should be in the regular route of
vessels, and, as the earliest course of sailors to the Gulf
of St. Lawrence was by the straits of Belle Isle, some
of the islands which shelter the harbours of Labrador
would probably have been the scene of the events
narrated. Jean Alphonse of Saintonge, who was Roberval's first pilot, no doubt indicates the island of our
heroine's trials under the name of *Isles de la Demoiselle*
in latitude 50·45, and he says there is a good harbour
there. This name clung for a long time to the
locality and is found on many old maps. To-day the
most important of the group is known as Grand
Meccatina Island.

SONNET.

O Love! thou art the soul's fixed star, whose light—
   A rapture felt through all the rolling years,—
   Absorbs with silent touch the mourner's tears,
A guide, a glory through our mortal night ;—
All other passions, be they dark or bright,
   All high desires are but thy subject spheres,
   And captive servitors, whose pathway veers,
Obedient to thine all-pervading might ;—
And therefore I no hesitation make
   In choosing thee, a theme accounted old,
Yet ever young, and for poor Marguerite's sake
I trust some kind remembrance to awake
   That shall in tenderest clasp her story hold,
   Even as a rose a drop of dew doth fold.

MARGUERITE

OR THE ISLE OF DEMONS,

The interior of a Convent in France: Group of Nuns
listening to Marguerite narrating her adventure.

1545.

PART I.

You ask me, Sisters, to relate
The story of the wanton fate
That over sea, with dole and strife
And love and hate enthralled my life,
Entwined with his, whose gentle eyes,
　　That never lost their winsome smile,
Illumed for me those sullen skies
　　Which canopy the haunted Isle,
A tale so wild, I pray you think,
　　May ill beseem and prove amiss

For such a hallowed place as this ;
A chain it is whose every link
Is rusted with some earthly stain,
The which you may esteem profane
And from its hapless wearer shrink,
I would not, Heaven knows, offend
The sanctity of sinless ears,
   Nor vex the pious soul that hears
Good angels on soft wings descend,
   Illumined, from the starry spheres,
To tread these cloistered aisles and bend
O'er dreaming couches lily pure.
But since your suffrance makes secure,
And since you kindly deign assent,
   And graciously with eager look
   Dispel the fluttering fears that shook
My contrite heart, I am content.

Ave Maria.

Mystic Mother ! who erewhile
Sought me on the Demons' Isle,
Sought, and with compassion mild
Shielded thy afflicted child ;

Shielded, and with vengeance new
Scattered the Satanic crew :
Blest Madonna! aid me now,
Lift the pressure from my brow ;
Bid the thunder-cloud depart
From my overladen heart ;
Tune my tongue, my lips inspire,
Touch them with celestial fire ;
Shape the lay as meet to set,
Like a modest violet,
In Saint Cecilia's coronet.

Three gallant ships that owned command
Of Roberval's imperial hand
Thundered to France a proud farewell
And sailed away from brusque Rochelle ;
Sailed on a breezy April day,
Sailed westward for a land that lay,
I heard the people wisely tell,
Betwixt the ocean and Cathay.
From shore to ship, from ship to shore
  A thousand parting signals flew ;
  Ah ! hopeful hearts, they little knew
That many were there who never more

Must see those faces that faded away,
And were lost in the distance cold and gray.
With troubled breast and tearful eye,
In fear and doubt, I knew not why—
   Unheedful of the sea-winds chill—
   I watched the land recede until
   The mountain peaks had passed from sight,
   Like clouds absorbed in morning's light,
   And ocean's border touched the sky.

Long backward, over leagues of foam,
   My greyhound gazed,—poor *Fida* knew
That he was borne afar from home,
   But not from friends, albeit few,
His still, for better days or worse,
His mistress and her Norman nurse.
   Far, out beyond the shining bay,
The sister vessels held their way,
Where, gifted with superior speed,
The " Royal Griffin " takes the lead,
As if she felt and understood
The stern old Viceroy's hasty mood.
   A man of courteous mien was he,
And smooth as any summer sea

When winds are laid ; he could be so
When naught befell to rouse the flow
Of passions that with scanty rest
Lay lava-like within his breast.
But Heaven fend or man or woman
　　Who set that fiery flood in motion ;—
　　His anger, like a storm-tossed ocean,
Was fearful in its rage ; no human
Expostulation, no appeal
Of speech, or tears, could make him feel
The benediction that is felt
　　By one whose soul, if prone to error,
Will yield at last and kindly melt,
　　And lay aside its robe of terror.
He could be calm, could well repress
His evil nature's fierce excess,
But only when upon him fell
　　The shadow of superior power,
　　Then like all tyrants he would cower
And play the courtier passing well.
But no superior save the king
　　Had he in all the land of France ;
　　In Picardy, his single glance
Was law, religion, everything.

His vassals prized his slightest nod,
And feared him more than fiend or God.
The modest maid, the peasant's bride
His foul approaches must not chide;
I blush, as if it were a sin,
To own him all too near of kin.
Seven sunny years had barely flown
    When I, an only child, was left,
    Of sire and happy home bereft,
To wipe a mother's tears alone.
A leader in the wars with Spain,
The hero whom we wept was slain.
Oh ! I remember well his look,
    His stature tall and noble brow,
Remember how he often strook
    And praised my long dark hair, and how
On that last morn of clouded bliss
He woke me with a parting kiss;
His hurried prayer, his slow farewell,
    The window flowers, the little room,
    The dangling sword, the nodding plume,
The long top-boots and shining spurs ;—
O, let this pass ! O, let me quell
    A memory shot through years of gloom.

My comely mother from the hour
  That chronicled his honoured death
Wilted and drooped, a pale sweet flower,
And three years gone I saw her breath
Grow faint and fail. Dear sainted mother !
  'Twas just before her spirit fled
She did beseech her lordly brother
  To shield her orphaned Marguerite's head.
He promised with a ready grace
  And in his rude capricious way
Thenceforth assigned me fitting place ;—
  But I was volatile and gay,
Ready of wit, of skilful hands,
  And minded not his curt commands.

Thus came to pass that on his ship,—
A ringdove in a falcon's grip,—
I sailed the surging seas afar.
But one was there, Eugene Lamar,
My bliss, my bane—I cared not what,
Who worshipped me, beside me sat,
And with me paced the giddy deck,
What time we watched the sea-mews peck
The foam that fringed the crested wave.

For me he ventured all, and gave
His fortune to the winds ; then why
Should aught disturb, or cause one sigh
To prophesy of lurking harm ?

Exultant in their new-found charm,
A motley throng of either sex,
    Of divers rank and variant age
Now promenade the oaken decks,
    Proud of an ocean pilgrimage.
We heeded not their boisterous glee,
    Their merry songs and dancing feet,
    Our happiness was too complete.
The azure sky and emerald sea,
    And free-born winds their magic wrought,
    Till every feeling, every thought,
Involved in tremulous ecstacy
    Made no account of sight or sound ;—
    We twain another world had found,
Whose warm excess of drowsing bliss
Excluded all the chills of this.

Our ship sped on, fresh blew the wind,
Her plodding mates lagged far behind ;

Like two white cloudlets waxing dim
They hung on the horizon's rim
For many days, but hull and mast
All wholly disappeared at last.

Mid-ocean crossed, the wind blew strong
And like a Nereid's dolorous song
Wailed through the rigging ; rose and fell
The billows with portentous swell.
Swift night came down, cold, wild and black,
Red lightnings lit the inky rack
Of hostile clouds ; a storm it grew,
And such a storm as men might rue.
The prince of air his bondage broke,
And loud in horrent thunder spoke ;
Our staunch craft felt the perilous strain,
And like a thing in mortal pain
Groaned audibly ; strong sails, though furled,
     Were rent in shreds
     From their ash spar beds
And wafted to some calmer world.

Two seamen from the yards were blown :
  An instant mid the tempest's roar,

Above the rattling thunder's tone,
   A double shriek was heard—no more !—
Their names, their fate, no stone records,
For them no consecrated words,
   Nor bell, nor candle ;—only this,
" Two mortals, to the world unknown
   Were blown into the salt abyss."
All night the elements beset
   Our hapless bark ; the mad waves leaped
   Like krakens on the deck, and reaped
A harvest which they garner yet.
Fierce down the hatchways snarled the sea,
   I heard the shout of Roberval
Command them closed ; ah me ! ah me !
   What prayers ! what shrieks ! I never shall,
   While memory marks the flight of years,
Forget that storm of phrenzied fears.
Think not our sex alone gave way
   To craven doubt and blanched despair ;—
Great burly men, whose heads were gray,
   Gave wildest wings to desperate prayer.
I dare believe they felt ashamed,—
The blessed Saints whose names were named
In phrase that seemed impiety.

What marvel if at such a time
  My lover groped his way to where
  My couch was spread, and tarried there?
Was such devotedness a crime?
Together on the floor we knelt
In quiet hopefulness, and felt
Assurance in our souls that He,
Who walked the waves of Galilee,
When, weak of faith and sore afraid,
The sinking Peter cried for aid,
Would manifest His sacred will;
  Would stretch His saving hand and bind
  The fury of the maddened wind,
And bid the savage waves be still.
My greyhound, ever near me, took
A painful and bewildered look;
All that dread night the narrow space
He traversed with unwearied pace.
The imminent danger well he knew,
And watched the changes of my face,
  And moaned at its unwonted hue.

The morn broke fair but other storm,
  More dreadful than the wrath of heaven,

2

Or rage of hell, began to form;
   The high-bred gossips, envy-driven
Did look askance, and whisper blame,
And young Lamar's and Marguerite's name
Were caught at, with but slight excuse,
As playthings for their wanton use.
Soon drifting round my uncle's ears
The idle tale in wrath he hears,
And starting from his proud repose
His fury like a whirlwind rose
And suddenly upon us burst.
I heard my name most foully curst
And coupled with a word of shame;
My tear-drenched cheeks grew all aflame;
Beside me, where I trembling stood,
   My watchful *Fida* whined and growled;
   The glaring maniac on him scowled,
His eyes two throbbing balls of blood,
And choking with some fiery word,
Drew forth and waved his gleaming sword,
Then smote the faithful brute;—his neck
Received the edge; athwart the deck
The severed head the slayer spurned:
   O God! I saw a sea of gore,

From which my eyes in horror turned ;—
   I swooned and recked of nothing more.
When from that death-like sleep I woke
   Lamar's moist eyes were near my face,
Some tender words he softly spoke,—
   My languid arms his neck embrace,
My lips their wonted banquet share,
And breathe again the vital air.
Ah ! never since that hour when whirled
Around with me a crimson world
Have I forgot or ceased to mourn
   The playmate of my childhood's years ;
   (Pardon, I pray, these silly tears.)
His long slim neck had often borne
My cheek, when tired with romping play
Under a chesnut's shade we lay,
His taper head flexed backward, till
His loving eyes had gazed their fill.

Harsh prelude this ! a warning fit
Of coming woes. The brow hard-knit,
The curling lip and heaving chest
Of Roberval presaged the rest.
But what his dark design might be

Eluded anxious scrutiny;
We only knew some purpose dire,
Like a swollen adder cirqued with fire,
Lay coiled within his vengeful heart,
Ready against our lives to dart.

    "Fear not, my love!" Eugene exclaimed,

    "Faint not, true heart! whose peace is spilt;
The evil tongues that have defamed

    Thy innocence shall own their guilt.
If blame there be 'tis I alone

    Have erred, nor do I shrink to bear
Thy kinsman's wrath, but how atone

    For wrong committed unaware?
Let unjust Roberval decree

    What punishment his ire may crave;
However tends his evil course,
He cannot, dearest one, divorce
My constant soul from thine—from thee,

    For even from the silent grave
I verily believe my love
Would issue through the cope above,
And mingling with the volant air
Pursue thy beauty alway, where
On any spot of land or sea

My Marguerite might chance to be."
His voice failed—tremulous, his eyes
Such passion held as well might save
A world from wreck; our wedded sighs
Made interlude to honied speech,
And bound us closer, each to each.

On flew the ship; a bounteous gale
Fed to repletion every sail,
And Tethys, turbulent no more,
  Advanced her banners, green and white,
  (In sooth it was a goodly sight)
Toward the wild Hesperian shore.
At length glad signs of land were seen,
  Strange birds, a friendly escort, came
  And perched upon the spars, so tame,
So numbed and wearied with the keen
Cold journey it had been no feat
To clasp their wings; but who could treat
Those little rovers of the sea,
That claimed our hospitality,
With less than Christian charity?

Westward across the ridgy waste
My uncle gazed as if in haste
To reach the promised port, but no !—
    His thought to other ends was set,
As soon the traitor meant to show.
With sudden stride, his hot brow wet
In oozing wrath, he gave command :
"Steer north-by-west !" The wonderland
Of Nurumbega hove in sight,
And outlined in a purple light
The dreaded *Isle of Demons* lay ;
Thither the *Griffin* bore away.
I saw the treacherous villain smile,
    And as the ship was drawing near
The marge of that unholy Isle
    I saw the sailors quake with fear.
A boat was launched, provisioned, stored
With arms and ammunition, oared
And quickly manned ;—for what ? for where
Let my false guardian's tongue declare.
"Go ! wretched girl," he fiercely said,
    As, from the ship, myself and nurse
    He hurried, " go, and take my curse,
All evil light upon thy head !

Hence to the *Demons' Isle*, a place
   Than which, save hell, there is no worse,
And ponder o'er thy rank disgrace ;
There only foul-faced devils dwell,
As every seaman here can tell.
Hence ! and prefer thy dainty charms
To glad some princely demon's arms.
Dishonour on my house, my name,
Confusion, everlasting shame,
Thou and thy paramour have wrought ;
For him, I swear he shall be taught
What torture means ;—the crippled crone
Who all your secret sins has known
And pandered to, let her partake
   The punishment assigned to you,
   A penance to such service due.
And when your threads of life shall break,
Then may you both for ages ache,
   Conjoined in purgatorial fires,
   Sure antidote to lewd desires."
His insults pierced like barbs of steel ;
   My patience I no longer nursed,
   I bade the tyrant do his worst :—
O, if he thought to see me kneel,

And for his mercy humbly sue,
'Twas little of his niece he knew ;
His curse, his terrors, I defied,
And told him in his teeth, he lied !
I even dared predict his fate ; (¹)
" Foredoomed," I said, " to all men's hate,
Like Cain or Judas thou shalt die
Unhoused, where none will pause to sigh
Denied the pity you deny."
He winced and wondered, powerless
    To check such unexpected scorn.
    A strength miraculous, new born
In uncontrollable excess,
From God or fiend I questioned not,
Through all my rigid being shot.
The boat received and swiftly bore
Its convicts to the fearful shore.
There all my fortitude departed,
And lorn and lost and broken-hearted
I stood upon the windy beach,
And stretched my hands as if to reach
The idol of my widowed soul.
" Farewell ! dear friend Eugene, farewell !
Those breakers that between us roll

Shall sound for me a fitting knell
When thou art borne I know not where."
Thus did my sorrow load the air.
He saw, he seemed to hear my wail,
And springing from the forward rail
Leapt in the sea, and bravely smote
    With lusty arms the foamy flood,
    Oh ! how my hot impetuous blood
Surged through my veins ; while still remote
He battled shoreward gallantly ;
    Now borne upon a toppling wave,
And blinded by the surfy spray,
Now lost to sight, now seen again,
While on the ship some fearless men
    Loud shouts of exultation gave ;
Then others into tumult broke,
Whose cheers the Island echoes woke.
But Roberval, whose stormy face
Flamed like a furnace, fiendish, base,
With levelled arquebuse took aim
Straight at the swimmer, shrieks of "Shame !"
He heeded not ; the bullets sped,
And whistled past my hero's head.
A few more strokes and he is safe !

The jagged rocks his strong limbs chafe,
But soon the slippery sands are gained
And I am to his bosom strained.
Their coifs the women, wild with gladness,
Stripped from their heads and, in their madness,
Flung to the waves, an offering fair
In witness of the Virgin's care,
My solace in the gulphs of sadness.
From stem to stern the furor ruled,
And Roberval, chagrined, befooled,
His sails reset, and sailed away,
   But half avenged; and we were left
   Of all the peopled world bereft,
To hell's dark brood a helpless prey.
But for that he I loved was still
Linked to my fate, for good or ill,
My thanks to gracious Heaven I wept.
The poor old nurse behind us crept,
And kneeling on the salty ground,
   A benediction even there,
   In answer to her silent prayer,
Deep in her withered heart she found.

The ship was gone, and with it went
　　All hope of ever seeing more
　　The glory of our native shore ;
I knew our cruel banishment
Was purposed for a lingering death,
A dirige of painful breath.
Was it in mercy he bestowed
The food and arms, a goodly load ?
Nay, these were meant to stretch the doom
That made the Isle an open tomb.
" Mourn not—sweetheart !" Eugene began,
" Here where the sea-winds rudely fan
Thy queenly brow, a queen to me
Henceforward thou shalt truly be ;
And if thou choose to reign alone
　　I'll be thy faithful paladin,
　　And many a noble trophy win
In honour of thy virgin throne.
Then come, while yet the lord of day
　　Dispenses light and gentle heat,
And let us hand and hand survey
　　The wonders of our new retreat.
　　This little kingdom, Marguerite !
Encircled by the shining sea,

Is large enough for thee and me."
'Twas thus in cheerful mood he sought
To lure the current of my thought
From cypress shades to run abroad
In pleasant ways, approved of God ;
Nor sought in vain : my spirit caught
The hue, the blessedness, the glow
That love's endearing words bestow,
And like a lark that sudden springs
From barren lands and soaring sings,
Rose heavenward on hopeful wings.

But hark ! the vesper *angelus*
In holy accents, tremulous,
Now calls us to the Virgin's shrine.
If still your wishes fair incline
To follow this capricious clue
　　To-morrow after open dawn
　　I'll join you on the eastern lawn,
Under the lindens, and pursue
My story to its tragic close.

PART II.

The tale continued in the Convent grounds; the
    same group of Nuns listening.

How softly have my limbs reposed !
    Nor stormy sea, nor haunted land,
    Nor sorcerer's unhallowed wand,
Disturbed the opiate shades that closed
    The sleepy avenues of sense ;
    And therefore I, without pretence
Of weariness or dream-wrought gloom,
My tale of yester-eve resume.

Together o'er the mystic Isle
We wandered many a sinuous mile.
'Twas midway in the month of June,
And rivulets with lisping rune,
And bowering trees of tender green,
And flowering shrubs their trunks between

Enticed our steps till gloaming gray
Upon the pathless forest lay.
Think not I journeyed void of fear ;
   Sir Roberval's hot malediction
Like hurtling thunder sounded near ;
Our steps the envious demons haunted,
   And peeped, or seemed to peep and leer,
   From rocky clefts and caverns drear.
But still defiantly, undaunted,
Eugene averred it had been held
By wise philosophers of eld
That all such sights and sounds are mere
Fantastic tricks of eye and ear,
   And only meet for tales of fiction.
" Heed not," he said, " the vicious threat,
   'Twas but a ruffian's empty talk,
The which I pray thou may'st forget
   And half his evil purpose baulk."
A silent doubt and grateful kiss
Was all I could oppose to this.
But firmer grew my steps.   The air
   Was laden with delicious balm ;
Rich exhalations everywhere,
   From pine and spruce and cedar grove,

And over all a dreamy calm,
    An affluence of brooding love,
A palpable, beneficent
Sufficiency of blest content.

Amid the hours, in restful pause
    We loitered on the moss-clad rocks,
And listened to the sober caws
    Of lonely rooks, and watched thick flocks
Of pigeons passing overhead ;
Or where the scarlet grosbeak sped,
    A wingéd fire, through clumps of pine
Sent chasing looks of joy and wonder.
    Blue violets and celandine,
And modest ferns that glanced from under
Gray-hooded boulders, seemed to say—
" O, tarry, gentle folk ; O, stay,
    For we are lonely in this wood,
And sigh for human sympathy
    To cheer our days of solitude."
Meek forest flowers, how dear to me !
    I loved them, kissed them on the stem,
And felt that I must ever be
    Secluded from the world like them.

The long-drawn shadows, eastward cast,
Admonished us that day was fast
Dissolving, and would soon be past ;
And we must needs regain the spot
   Where waited good Nanette our coming.
The chattering squirrel we heeded not,
   Nor paused to list the partridge drumming.
The wedded bird was in her nest,
   And knew from the suspended song
(A tribute to her listening ear)
That from the green boughs rustling near
   Had trilled and warbled all day long,
A brief space only must she wait
The fondling of her chirping mate.
With some wise meaning, wise and deep
That from her eyes was fain to peep,
And wealth of words and lifted hands
   Our thoughtful servitor, Nannette,
   Gave kindly greeting ere we met.
" Come, children, follow me," she said,
And silently the way she led
   An arpent from the ocean sands,
Directly to a piny grove,
Where she with wondrous skill had wove

A double bower of evergreen,
Meet for a fairy king and queen.—
" There, tell your rosaries and take
A sabbath slumber ; till you wake,
Nannette, hard by, will watchful stand,
With loaded arquebuse in hand,
Your trusty sentinel, for here
Some prowling beast may chance appear
On no good neighbour's lawful quest ;
To-morrow I can doze and rest."—
Thus, voluble, my faithful Nurse.

Amazed, I stood and could not speak,
But kissed her on the brow and cheek,
And wept to think my Uncle's curse
Should fall on her, so worn and bent,
So moved with every good intent.

A flushing joy it was to see
That double-chambered arbour fair,
Re-calling to my memory
The storied lore of things that were
My childhood's moonlit witchery.
Next morn we sought the circling strand
And question made of wind and sea

If such a thing might ever be,
That, soon or late, from any land
Some friendly sail would come that way
    And waft us thence : in vain, in vain !
The hollow wind had nought to say,
    But, like a troubled ghost, passed by ;—
The waste illimitable main
    And awful silence of the sky
Vouchsafed no sign, made no reply.—
Oft times upon some lifted rock
    That overhung the waves, we sate
And listened to the undershock
    Whose sad persistency, like fate,
    Made land and sea more desolate.

Again in lighter mood we trod
The yellow sands and pale-green sod
Strewn with innumerable shells,
In whose pink whorls and breathing cells
Beauty and wonder slept enshrined,
Like holy thoughts in a dreamer's mind.
Of these sea-waifs an ample store
We gathered, and at twilight bore
The treasure to our sylvan home.

Once more the star encumbered dome
Of heaven its thrilling story told,
And Dian, lovely as of old,
Poured lavishly her pallid sheen
Upon that tranquil world of green ;
Whose cool and dewy depths, now rife
With luminous and noiseless life,
Responded wide ; the fire-fly race
  In myriads lit their tiny lamps ;
  As an army's countless camps
The warder in some woody place
At nightfall on his watch may trace ;
  So gleamed and flashed those mimic lamps.

The third day came.   From shore to shore,
Adventurous ever more and more,
Our penal Isle we wandered o'er.—
Which way our roving fancy led,
A wilding beauty largely spread
Rewarded our ambitious feet,
And made our banishment too sweet
For further censure or repining.
  Now culling flowers of dainty dyes,
  Now chasing gaudy butterflies,

And now on herbaged slopes reclining,
Where purple blooms of lilac trees,
And sultry hum of hermit bees
Disarmed the hours of weariness.—
Nor can you fail, dear friends, to guess
   That time for dalliance we found,—
And if we loved to an excess
In many a long involved caress,
   O think how we were cribbed and bound.—
Lush nature and necessity,
   As witnessed by the Saints above,
   In one delicious circle wove
The pulsings of our destiny.

The great rude world was far away,
And like a troubled vision lay
Outside our thoughts ; its cold deceits,
The babble of its noisy streets,
And all the selfish rivalry
That courts and castles propagate
Were alien to our new estate.—
A fragment of propitious sky,
Whereon a puff of cloud might lie,
Through verdured boughs o'er-arching seen,

And glimpses of the sea between
Far stretches of majestic trees,
Such peaceful sanctities as these
Were our abiding joyance now.

Cheerily and with lifted brow
Eugene led on, where tamaracs grew,
And where tall elms their shadows threw
Athwart a little glen wherein
A virgin brook seemed glad to win
The pressure of our thirsty lips.
    Pleasant it was to linger there
And cool our fevered finger-tips
    In that pellucid stream and share
The solace of the ocean breeze.
    For summer heats were now aglow,
The fox sat down and took his ease,
    The hare moved purposeless and slow ;
But louder rang the blue jay's scream,
    The woodpeck tapped the naked tree,
    Nor ceased the simple chicadee
To twitter in the noonday beam.—

My lover, wheresoe'er we strayed,
   Made search in every charmed nook,
   And angled in the winding brook
For all sweet flowers that love the shade
To twine for me a bridal braid.
Pale yellow lillies, nursed by rocks
Rifted and scarred by lightning shocks,
Or earthquake ; river buds and pinks,
   And modest snow-drops, pearly white,
   And lilies of the vale unite
Their beauty in close-loving links
Around a scented woodbine fair
To coronate my dark brown hair.
The fragile fern and clover sweet
On that enchanted circlet meet ;
Young roses lent their blushing hues,
Nor could the cedar leaf refuse
With helmet flowers to intertwine
Its glossy amplitude divine.—
Emerging from that solemn wood,
High on a rocky cliff we stood
At set of sun ; far, far away
The splendors of departing day
Upon the barren ocean lay.—

There on that lone sea-beaten height,
Investured in a golden light,
Eugene, with looks half sad, whole sweet,
Upon my brow the garland set,
At once a chaplet and aigrette,
And said : "Be crowned, my Marguerite !
My own true soul, my ever dear
    Companion in this wilderness.
Though hopeful still, I sometimes fear
    That days of darkness and distress
May come to thee when woods are sere,—
When it may baffle all my skill
To guard thee from white winter's chill ;—
But hence all raven-thoughts of ill,
Let me believe that Nature will
Relax her rigour, having caught
    The soft infection of those eyes
    In whose blue depths my image lies,
Even as my soul, with love distraught,
Like a lone star drowned in the sea,
Is wholly drowned and lost in thee.—
Love is our own essential being,
    Sole sovereign over utmost fate,
Its own sufficient laws decreeing,

MARGUERITE.

Immortal and immaculate ;
And when this mild ethereal flame
To mortal man was kindly given
'Twas surely meant by highest Heaven
That never aught of evil name
Should dare attempt to thwart its power.—
Then let us, dearest, from this hour
Defy the future, and pursue
The unimagined pleasure due
To such surpassing love as ours.
One moment in thy folding arms
Alone in these sequestered bowers ;
One throb of thy impassioned heart,
Now speaking audibly to mine,
And saying, " It were death to part ; "
One honey-dew caress of thine,
Out-sums a million rude alarms,
Out-lives whole centuries that weigh
On loveless souls, on sordid clay,
That gravitate to ways of shame,
And know love's magic but by name.—
These roseate skies will change their hue ;
This pomp of leaves when autumn lowers
The windy ways of earth will strew ;

This aromatic crown of flowers,
Made sacred now since worn by you,
To-morrow will begin to fade.—
    But love, sweet spirit, linked as ours,
By sad vicissitude o'erlaid,
Endures, unchanged by any breath
    Of adverse fate, and surely will
    Life's last inevitable chill
Survive, and triumph over death."—
    Thus, eloquent, the radiant youth,
Like one inspired with sacred truth,
Fair as Adonis, o'er me breathed
The incense of pure love, and wreathed
My heart in dewy dreams of bliss.
    Consenting Nature, pleased the while,
    Bestowed upon her outcast Isle
    The magic of a mother's smile.
Spent Sol impressed his warmest kiss
On ocean's brow ; the wanton wind
Went sighing up and down to find
    Meet objects for his soft embrace
All things to amity inclined ;
    Fierce bird and beast forebore to chase
Their feeble prey, as if they felt

Love's universal breathings melt
Their savage instincts ; everywhere,
Like mute enchantment in the air,
This subtle permeating power
Reigned sole.   O, blest ambrosial hour !
O, halcyon days that followed after,
With music from my lute, and laughter,
And song and jest, and such full measure
Of secret love's exhaustless treasure
As gave to pain the wings of pleasure !—

So fled our summer dream, as flies
An angel through cerulean skies
   On some good errand swiftly bent,
So brief its stay that ere we wist,
Gruff Autumn, garmented in mist.
   His courier winds before him sent,
The which, equipped with sleet and hail,
Beat down as with an iron flail
The grandeur of the woods, and left
Their naked solitudes bereft
Of bird and flower.   The trees stood stark
And desolate against the dark
Chaotic sky.   The mighty sea

Its billows hurled upon the shore
As if resolved to over-pour
And gulph our prison-house.   Ah, me !
All roofless now, save here and there
A tall pine stretched its spear-shaped head
Aloft into the gelid air ;
The hemlock, too, its beauty spread,
A tent-like pyramid of green,
Symbols of hope amid a scene
Where hope grew pale at winter's tread.

No more, along the sounding shore,
In hushed voluptuous dells, no more,
Nor on the perilous rock which gave
Rude welcome to the climbing wave,
Might we, in amplitude of joy,
Our paradisal hours employ,—
From green to gray, from gray to white,
So rapidly the change came on,
It seemed but the work of a single night
And all our faery world was gone.—
Down came the snow, compact, hard-driven
By all the scourging blasts of heaven,
Until, like clouds, dethroned and hurled

Tumultuous to this nether world,
Around the desert isle it lay,
A rampart to the ocean's spray.

Half hid where friendly pine trees spread
Perpetual shelter overhead,
Hugging a hillside lifted high
Betwixt us and the arctic sky,
Our cabin stood ; a poor defence
Against the mute omnipotence
Of searching and insidious frost,
Which, like a ghoul condemned and lost,
The closeness of an inmate claimed ;—
But on the rustic hearthstone flamed
Dry wood and pine-knots resinous :
    A ready and abundant hoard
    When days were long our hands had stored
Against the season perilous ;
And good Nanette, 'twas her desire
To feed the bickering tongues of fire
That warned the dumb intruder hence.

When night fell thick, I loved to sit
And watch the fire-gleams fall and flit

On wooden walls and birch-bark ceiling,
Among the densest shadows stealing,
Till these, in folds and festoons golden,
Like tapestry of castles olden,
Shifted and fluttered free, revealing
To fancy's charmed and wiser vision
Such fabrics as in looms elysian
The angels weave ; and thus our hut
A palace seemed ; and was it not
More beautiful, illumed the while
By dear Eugene's adoring smile,
Than many a royal chamber where,
Concealed amid the gloss and glare,
A thousand hateful evils are ? —

Such fare as woodland wilds afford,
Supplied our ever-cheerful board ;
Nor such alone ; the salt sea wave
Its tributary largess gave,
All that our lenten wants might crave.

Slow crept the whitened months, so slow—
    I sometimes felt I never more
 Should see the pretty roses blow,

Or tread on aught but endless snow,
  And listen to the nightly roar
Of tempest and the ocean flow.
Weird voices, woven with the wind,
Riding on darkness often came
And syllabled the buried name
Of Roberval, which, like a hearse,
Bore inward to my palsied mind
The ghost of his inhuman curse.

Was it sick fancy, sore misled,
That to my shuddering spirit said ?—
" Those sounds that shake the midnight air,
Are threats of Shapes that will not spare
Your trespass on their fief accurst."
  " Hush, hush, my love," Eugene would say,
" That cry which o'er our cabin burst,
  Came from the owls, perched royally
Among the pine-tops ; you but heard
The language of some beast or bird ;
The mooing of a mother bear,
An hungered in her frozen lair ;
The laugh and mooing of the loon
That welcometh the rising moon.

The howling of the wolves you hear,
In chase of some unhappy deer,
Impeded in its desperate flight
   By deep and thickly crusted snows,
   O'er which its lighter-footed foes
Pursue like shadows of the night.
That lengthened groan, that fearful shriek
Was but the grinding stress and creak
Of aged trees; they seem to feel
The wrench of storms, and make appeal
For mercy; in their ducts and cells
The sap, which is their life-blood, swells
When frosts prevail and bursts asunder
With sharp report its prison walls;
Then cease, beloved, to fear and wonder
   For all these harmless peals and calls.
In sweet assurance rest, love, rest
Thy head on this devoted breast,
And dream sweet dreams; the gentle spring
Will come anon, and birds will sing
As sweetly as they sang last year;
And shall I not be ever near
To share with thee the murmuring
Of waking life? the humble bee

Will drone again as blissfully
As when from flower to flower he went
And to the choral symphony
His basso horn serenely lent."—
My fears were laid ; I ceased to think ;
Athirst and eager still to drink
The nectar of his speech.

                              How oft,
   If he but chanced to hear me sigh
When wild winds blew, or when the soft
   And flaky harvest of the sky
Descended silent, he would sit
   Under that snow-thatched roof and tell
Such marvellous tales of mirth and wit,
   They held me like a wizard's spell.
Or else some poet's plaintive verse
   That breathed soft vows of youth and maiden,
   Witn love-begotten sorrow laden,
In twilight tones he would rehearse ;
And whilst the rhythmic measure flowed
   From those attuned lips, my breast
With trepidation heaved and glowed,
   For in such guise was well expressed

The master-passion's undertone,
  Or happy or disconsolate,
  Of many a lover's wayward fate
That bore some semblance to our own.

'Twere over-much to pause and tell
How slid the weeks, and all befell
Ere we could to the heavens say,
  " The terror of your rage is past,
  The gnawing frost, the biting blast,
And life is in the matin ray."—
The swallow came, the heron's scream
  Athwart the marsh-lands, through the woods,
Sped resonant ; I ceased to dream
  Of demons, and my waking moods
The radiance of the morning took.
Upon the bare brown leaves I stood,
  And saw and heard with raptured look
  The gleam and murmur of the brook,
Which we in summer's plenitude
  Had traced to many an arbored nook.

'Twas midmost in the budding May,
  Whilst on my couch of cedar boughs,
4

Perturbed with nameless fears I lay,
  And breathed to Heaven my silent vows,—
A cloud-like cope of purple hue
  Descended o'er me, hid me quite,
And seemed a soft wind round it blew,
And from the mystic wind a voice
  Spoke low : " Poor child of darkened light !
The pure of heart are Heaven's choice ;
The Virgin who hath seen thy tears,
In pity for thy tender years,
Will aid thee in thine utmost plight."
A hallowed tremor o'er me crept,
And in that purple cloud I slept
Enshrined, how long I never knew ;—
And through my dreams the soft wind blew
Like music heard at dusk or dawn,
And when I woke and found it gone,
In fullness of great joy I wept.

'Twas thus a new revealment came,
  A something out of nothingness,
To which we gave the simple name
  Of Lua.   O, the first caress
A mother to her first-born gives !—

Methinks the angels must confess,
Through all the after ages' lives,
An influence so pure and holy,
That human hearts, the proud and lowly,
Are touched thereby.   I kissed, and kissed
My pretty babe, and through the mist
Of happy tears upon it gazed
In silent thankfulness, and praised
The Empress of the skies, whose grace
Had glorified that humble place.

The sandy marge again we trod
Round the green Isle, and felt that God
Was very near,—in ocean's roar,
   And in the zephyr's scented breath,
In summer green, in winter hoar,
   In joy, in grief, in life, in death,
Our Friend and Father evermore.

Again across the naked sea,—
   In tumult or in blank repose,
   At morn and noon, and evening close,—
Sick yearnings from our souls were sent.
   But bootless still the hungry sigh,

A southward sail still southward went,
   If any such we might descry,—
As twice or thrice it chanced to be,
We saw or fancied shimmering,
Like a white eagle's outstretched wing,
Hiding the strait and dubious space
That separates the lifted face
   Of ocean from the stooping sky.
The sail would melt, the hollow dome
Above us and our prison home,
And girdling waves, and sobbing rain,
   And winds full-fledged,—all things that were
   Of earth and sky, of sea and air,
   Strangled sweet Hope, and in the pit
   Of outer darkness buried it.
Yet seemed it sinful to complain,
When to our feast of love was given
The fairest fruit that gracious Heaven
Had e'er for human joyance shed.
Sweet Innocence ! the small hands spread,
Dimpled and white, catching at things
   Viewless to us, but clearly seen
By those wide-open eyes ; the wings
   Of heavenly guests it must have been

Fluttering near the sinless child,
Azure and golden, till she smiled
   And shrank from their excessive sheen.

Again the forest's green arcades
Gladly we paced ; their sunlit shades
Investured us ; the laughing brook
   That solaced us the year before,
Mirrored again my lingering look ;
In that clear glass I could not fail
To see my face grown somewhat pale,
   But not less fair ; we trod once more
The lofty cliff whereon Eugene
Had crowned me his bride and queen.
Pleasant those summer days to walk
Where no intrusive step could baulk
Our happiness ; no tongue to dare
Whisper disparagement, and bare
The mysteries of Love's free-will,
Approved of Heaven to strive for still,
The liberty that angels share.—
Another summer's beauty dead,
   Another winter's cerements wound
   On tree and shrub ; the sheeted ground,

The cruel storm-land overhead,
The scream of frightened birds, the wind
   That in its teeth the tree-tops took
   And worried all day long and shook,
These and the monstrous ocean blind
With foamy wrath, were ours once more ;—
   Once more within our cabin mewed
Under the pine tops, crisp and hoar,
   My fears their old alarms pursued.

Four times the moon had waxed and waned
   Since summer blooms, so bright and brief,
   Were mourned for by the falling leaf,
And winter winds were all unchained,
When came the direful, fatal day.
   The Spectre of the wide world came
In league with winter's fierce array,
   In league with fiends that hissed the name
Of Death around the ruined Isle.

Deep lay the snow, pile heaped on pile,
When food fell scant, and on a morn,
Ere yet the infant light was born,
Eager-thus alway to provide,

Eugene forsook my drowsy side,
And lavished on my happy lips
His silent love; then gently slips,
Upon the little callow heap
That lay embalmed in downy sleep
His softest kisses : happy child !
She made a little stir and smiled,
As if in soothest dreams she knew
Whence came that quiet fond adieu.
Then pausing at the windy door,
    His arquebuse on shoulder laid,
    And in his belt a shining blade,
His brow a troubled shadow wore;—
Or was it but my own blurred thought
A semblance of foreboding wrought?
Backward he moved, a tardy pace,
And toward me turned his comely face
And said : " Dear love, I thought to go
Ere thou shouldst wake, for well I know
These frequent partings, though but brief,
Aye touch thy tender heart with grief."
" Loud blows the nor-wind," I replied.
    " Surely thou needst not haste away
    Before the leaden eyes of Day

On our small world are opened wide ;
For all these partings, my Eugene,
Are bitter drops that fall between
Our honied draughts of happiness ;
   Ah ! well I know what dangerous toil,
What weary hours companionless,
   Are thine in quest of needful spoil,
Be-wrenched, from stubborn wood and wave,
Wherein—Oh God !—an early grave
May compass thee ; and I remain
   A wretched mourner, doomed to bear
The burning curse and bitter bane
   Bequeathed me by Sir Roberval ;—
   O stay, Eugene, stay yet awhile !
Just now I dreamt I saw thee borne
By Shapes unshapely, stark and shorn,
   Three times around the darkened Isle ;
Then did the heavens o'er thee bend,
And in a cloud thou didst ascend,
Lost to the world and me forever."
   " Twas but a dream," he said, " no more,"
But saying which, a painful quiver
   His lips betrayed, then cheerily bore
His manly head, and thus made end.

" No evil can such dreams portend :—
Nor need I, dearest, say farewell ;
  For love and faith cannot deceive,
  And hence I cannot but believe,
What holy whispers round me tell,
That though thou tarriest here behind,
  Thy spirit journeyeth with me,
  Clasping me round whereso I be,
A shelter from the bruising wind,
  A covert from the drenching sea.
Then rest, my own brave Marguerite,
  Rest thee in trust ; 'tis meet that I
  The savage elements defy
For thy loved sake, and for the sweet,
Sweet sake of her who slumbers there,
Pillowed upon her golden hair,
Her beauty, love, so like thine own ;—
  Sweet babe ! dear wife !" Ere I could speak
  He kissed the tear-drop from my cheek,
And ere I wist I was alone,
  The door stood wide, and he had passed
  Into the dusky void, and vast
Uncertainties concealed by Fate.
Ah, me ! I could but watch and wait

For his return.   For his return?
I felt my heart within me burn,
Then sicken to an icy dread,
For seemed a sad voice near me said,
" Thou ne'er shall see his face again ! "
The paragon of noblest men !
It could not be ; I would not own
A prophecy that turned to stone
All joys that I had ever known.

The wind increased, the day wore on,
And ere the hour was half-way gone
That follows noon, a storm of snow
Blinded the heavens, and denser grew,
    And fiercer still the fierce wind blew
As night approached, a night of woe,
    Such as no fiend might add thereto.

The double darkness walled us in,
    The blackness of the storm and night,
And still he came not ! O, what sin,
    What blasphemy against the light
Of Heaven had my soul committed?
    Never before had eventide

Once found him absent from my side.
Eugene came not ! deceived, outwitted,
  Sore tempest-tossed and lured astray.
By demons, when the night-owl flitted
  Across his face at close of day,
Groping for home, exhausted, faint,
No angel near, no pitying saint
  To aid his steps and point the way.

From ebb of day till noon of night,
And onward till return of light,
The signal horn, Nanette and I,
Alternate blew, but for reply
The wind's unprecedented roar,
And ocean thundering round the shore
Our labor mocked ; and other sounds,
Nor of the land, nor sea, nor sky,
Our ears profaned ; the unleashed hounds
Of spleenful hell were all abroad,
And round our snow-bound cabin trod,
And stormed on clashing wings aloof,
And stamped upon the yielding roof,
And all our lamentation jeered.

Down the wide chimney-gorge they peered
   With great green eye-balls fringed with flame;—
The holy cross I kissed and reared,
   And in sweet Mary's blessed name,
Who erst had buoyed my sinking heart,
Conjured the foul-faced fiends depart.
Their shriekings made a storm more loud
Than that before whose fury bowed
The hundred-ringéd oaken trees ;
More fearful, more appalling these
Than thunder from the thunder-cloud ;
But trembling at the sacred sign,
And mention of the Name divine,
They dared not, could not disobey,
But fled in baffled rage away.—

The morrow came, and still the morrow,
But neither time, nor pain, nor sorrow,
Nor any evil thing could make
My stricken soul advisement take
Of aught that in the world of sense
The fiat of Omnipotence
Might choose prescribe ; I only know
That fever came, whose fiery flow

Surged through the temple-gates of thought,
Till merciful delirium wrought
Release from knowledge, from a world
Where Death's black banner stood unfurled.—

Restored—condemned—to conscious life,
The parting hour, the storm, the strife,
Rose from their tombs and dimly passed,
But on my spirit only cast
A feeble shade.   When known the worst,
When every joy that love has nursed
Lies cold and dead, a sullen calm
Sheds on the bleeding heart a balm
That is not peace, and does not heal,
But makes it half content to feel
    The frost upon the withered leaf,
To see love's lifeboat rock and reel
    And founder on the stormy reef.

A languid stupor, chill and gray,
Upon my listless being lay—
I knew and felt Eugene was not ;—
I saw that in the osier cot,
Constructed by his cunning skill,

My babe lay sleeping, very still :
So very still and pale was she,
That when I questioned, quietly,
How long since she had fallen asleep,
Nanette could only moan and weep,
And rock her body to and fro.—
With cautious step, and stooping low,
I took the little dimpled hand
    In mine, and felt the waxen brow.

    O, Queen of Heaven ! clearly now,
'Twas given me to understand
That all the warmth of life had fled ;
My babe, my pretty babe, was dead !—
In stupefaction fixed I stood
    Smitten afresh ; a wailing cry,
The wounded love of motherhood,
    Rose from my heart ; mine eyes were dry
Denied the blessed drops that give
A little ease, that we may live—
Live on, to feel with every breath
That life is but the mask of death.

Regardful of my frozen gaze,
    Hard set upon the frozen face,

Nannette, at length, in halting phrase,
   Her painful pass essayed to trace:
Told how, when hot the fever ran
Along my veins, and when the wan
And wasted moonshine fringed the hearth,
And voices that were not of earth
Came through the gloom, the famished child,
With pouting lips and eyelids mild,
Her wonted nourishment did crave;
And how, O God forgive ! she gave
The little mouth its wish.   She told
How dismal were the nights and cold,
Her haunted hours of rest how few,
And how my precious darling drew
From the distempered fevered fount
   The malady that raged in me.
How long it was, the tangled count,
   One week or two, or maybe three—
Her head astray, she could not tell,
When rang, she said, a silvery bell,
A-tolling softly far away.
   So softly tolling, faint and far,
   When quiet as the morning star,
That cannot brook the glare of day,

And seeks the upper azure deep,
My Lua (pardon if I weep),
Pure nestling of this sinful breast,
Had struggled into gracious rest.

Unhappy nurse ! that hallowed knell
Which on her pious fancy fell
Through midnight dreams was solace meet
For one whose slow, uncertain feet
Their journey's end had well-nigh gained ;
Whose meagre face drooped, pinched and pained,
From ague-fits that lately shook
All gladness from its kindly look.
No longer in those furrows played
The gleams of mirth that erst had made
Her gossip by the cabin fire,
A pleasing hum ; for she had store
Of gruesome tales and faery lore,
Which suited with the elfin quire
Of winds that on the waste of night.
Their voices spent ; 'twas her delight,
In calmer hours, her voice to strain
  With lays of roving Troubadour
That from her girlhood's bloom had lain

Mid memory's tuneful cords secure.
How changed she was ! soon, soon I felt
My pity for her dolour melt.
My friend and sole companion now,—
I brushed the gray hairs from her brow
And kissed it ; then came back to me
The days when on that palsied knee
I perched, a happy child ; where late
My babe, my second self had sate :—
Strange orbiting of time and fate.
Hid in the upheaved scarp of rock
That screened our hut from winter's shock
A cave there was of spacious bound,
Wherein no wave of human sound
Had ever rolled ; imprisoned there,
Like a grey penitent at prayer,
Hoar Silence wept, and from the tears
  Embroidered hangings, fold on fold,
  And silver tassels tinct with gold
The fingering of the voiceless years
Had deftly wrought, and on the walls
In sumptuous breadth of foamy falls
The product of their genius hung.
  From floor to ceiling, arched and high—

A counterfeited cloudy sky,—
Smooth alabaster pillars sprung.
On either side might one espy
What seemed hushed oratories rare
Inviting sinful knees to prayer.

Into that chapel-like retreat,
Untrod before by human feet,
The wicker cot, wherein still lay
My Lua's uncorrupted clay
We bore, and in an alcove's shade
Our tear-dewed burthen softly laid.
Long muffled in my heavy woe,
　　I knelt beside the little bed
　　And many a tearful Ave said.
At length, at length, I rose to go,
But kneeling still, my poor Nanette,
Her crucifix and beads of jet
Clasped in her praying hands, stirred not,
　　Nor spoke ;—our flickering lamp
　　Through the sepulchral gloom and damp
Made sickly twilight round the cot.
Orbed in her upturned hollow eyes
Two tear-drops gleamed.　I said, "Arise!

Come, come away.   Good sister, come !."
Still motionless as death and dumb,—
I shook her gently, spoke again,
    When sudden horror and affright
Laid hold upon my reeling brain ;
    Her soul, unshrived, had winged its flight !—
I sank upon the clammy stone,
The lamp died out and all was night.
" Mother of God I alone I alone I "
    I cried in agonized despair,
    " O pity me I O Mary spare !
A mother's anguish hast thou known,
O pity me ! alone ! alone I "
A thousand startled echoes sprang
Forth from their stony crypts, and rang
A ghostly miserere round
The cavern's dread Cimmerian bound,
Till sinking to a dying moan
They answered back, " alone ! alone I "

" Nay, not alone, poor Marguerite I "
I heard a voice divinely sweet,
And in a moment's awful space
That silent subterranean place

Was filled with light ;—I did not dream :
In beauty and in love supreme,
Before me shone our Lady's face.
(O would I could behold it now)
The coronal upon her brow,
With star-like jewels thickly set,
   The Sovereign presence certified.
Pure as the snow that lingered yet
   On solemn heights, with sunrise dyed,
Her raiment gleamed. " Weep not," she said,
   And toward me stretched her sacred hands
As if to raise my drooping head ;
   " Be comforted ! the triple bands
      Of grief and pain
Which Death around thy heart has coiled
      Shall part in twain ;
If secret sin thy soul hath soiled,
If thou thy lover loved too well,
The Seraphs say in high debate,
' Better excessive love than hate,
      Save hate of hell.'
If fiends infest this desert Isle
   Regard them not ; the soul whose trust
On Heaven leans, may calmly smile

At Satan's utmost stretch of guile
   And tread down evil things like dust.
The working of the wicked curse
Branded upon thyself and nurse
Shall cease with dawn of hallowed days ;
   She fitting sepulture hath found
   Under and yet not under ground ;
   Here leave her kneeling by the child,
Here, where the power thy God displays
   Shall keep their bodies undefiled,
Shall change to marble, flesh and bone.
Then come, and leave the dead alone ;
Come hence !—thy round of days complete,
Thy babe and lover shalt thou meet
      In Paradise.
      Look up, arise !
My hands will guide thy fainting feet."
She led me to the outer light,
   And ere a second breath I drew,
   Ere I could fix my dazzled view,
She vanished from my misted sight.

Resigned, uplifted, forth I went,
But, oh ! 'tis hard to nurse content

In silent walls ; to ever meet
With filling eyes the vacant seat ;
To tread from day to day alone
The silent ways, familiar grown,
Where dear companionship has shed
A glory and a rapture fled ;
Where every hillock, tree and stone
Are memories of a loved one, dead !

Again the flowering springtime came,
   The wedding-time of happy birds,
But not, oh ! not for me the same ;
   To whom could I address fond words ?
The violet and maple leaf,
Had they but known my wintry grief,
They would not have appeared so soon.
   I could not bear to look upon
   The beauty of the kindling dawn,
Nor sunset, nor the rising moon,
   Nor listen to the wooing notes
   That warbled from a thousand throats,
From cool of morn till heat of noon.
My soul was with the wind that sighed
Among the tree-tops ; all the wide

Waste desolation of the sea
Possessed me ; I could not agree
With aught of earth or firmament.
Where could I go ? which way I went
His melancholy shade did glide
Behind the rocks, among the trees,
And whispered in the twilight breeze
Endearments whispered long ago.
 In constancy of love and fear
 My sick heart bore his heavy bier,
How lovingly the angels know.

I knew not of my lost love's tomb,
Whether amid the shrouding gloom
Of some tenebrous yawning chasm,
Or in the watery world's abysm,
He met those spectres of my dream ;
No trace, no sign, no faintest gleam
Did all my questing ever show.
'Twas well, perchance, that this was so ;
But may I not believe that yet,
Long after we again have met,
I shall know all ? shall hear him tell
What on that dreadful night befell,

And how when in the toils of death
He called me with his latest breath
And blessed me? It will magnify
The joys of that dear home on high
If memory keep our bygone woe,
Our grievings of this world below.

A huntress of the woods I grew,
  Necessity my frailty taught
To track the fleetest quarry through
The forest, wet with morning dew,
  Unheedful of the bruises wrought
On tender feet; the wounds received
From thorns whose leafy garb deceived
My glowing limbs. My loosened hair
  I freely gave to every wind,
  Content to feel it stream behind,
Or drift across my bosom bare.

So passed the uneventful days,
The sad monotony of weeks,
Till August suns had ceased to blaze;
  Till o'er the forest's hectic cheeks
A languishing and slumbering haze,

The mellow Indian Summer crept ;
It was as if chaste Dryads wept
At sign of Winter's coming tread,
Till from their falling tears was spread
Those exhalations o'er the woods
Amid whose greenest solitudes
Their festivals of joy they kept.

So came the Autumn's ruddy prime,
And all my hopes, which had no morrow,
Like sea-weed cast upon the beach,
Like drift-wood barely out of reach
Of waves that were attuned to sorrow,
Lay lifeless on the strand of time.

So ebbed my life till beamed the hour
When burst in sudden bloom the flower
Of merciful deliverance.
That day I walked as in a trance,
My dismal round, as was my wont,
To many a joy forsaken haunt
Where oft upon my lover's breast
My head had lain in blissful rest,
Till coming to that sea-beat height

Where erst, enrobed in golden light,
His hands, aglow with love, conferred
   Upon my brow the spousal wreath,
   Whilst heaven and all things underneath
His words of sweet adorement heard.
There failed my limbs, and long I sate
At one with thoughts grown desperate.
Two winters had I known since first
I stood upon that Isle accurst,
The third a near, and how could I
Its killing frosts and snows defy ?
Surely 'twere better now to die.
So ran my thoughts, and fair in sight
The breakers tossed their plumes of white,
The same as on that fearful day
When bravely through their blinding spray
My menaced lover fought his way.
I listened to their luring speech
Till lost in lornest fantasy ;
Till toward me they did seem to reach
White jewelled hands to join with mine.
I rose and answered : " I am thine,
Thou desolate and widowed Sea,
That late hath come to pity me.

My lost Eugene ! 'neath yonder wave
  Oh should thy faithful Marguerite
  Thy lonely corse in darkness meet
How calm, how blest will be my grave !
Sweet babe, adieu ! and thou, Nannette,
With tearful eyes on Heaven set,
Thy watch beside my Lua keep."
Forward I stepped, prepared to leap ;—
One loving thought, one hasty glance
Sent o'er the deep to sunny France,
When hove directly into view
A sail, a ship ! could it be true ?
Or but a phantom sent to mock
My madness on that lonely rock ?
Agape I stood with staring eyes
An instant, then my frantic cries
Went o'er the deep, they heard, they saw,
Those mariners, and from the maw
Of Death my timely rescue made.
  My Country's flag the good ship bore,
And just as day began to fade
  We parted from that fatal shore,
And long ere moonrise many a mile
To northward loomed the Demon's Isle.

Soon, homeward bound, again I trod
My native soil, and thanked my God
For that on me he deigned to smile.

Here ends my tale.   And now, I pray,
If I have stumbled on the way,
Have shown but little tuneful skill
In this wild chant of good and ill,
My faults, my frowardness forgive.
Here, a sad vestal, let me live,
And share with you the peaceful bliss
That points a better world than this ;
Here shall I seek from Heaven to win
Forgiveness for my days of sin ;
Here shall my soul in prayer ascend
For him I loved ; my godlike friend,
My Husband ! if that honored name
Is due to one who naught of blame,
No falsehood, no unmanly art
Ere harbored in his open heart,
Then truly can nor ban nor bar
Deny it to the lost Lamar.
And if at times his spirit flits,
    Even here within this holy place,

With mournful eyes before my face,
And by my couch in silence sits
Till blooms the morn, I dare not pray
The gentle shade to haste away.

(1) NOTE TO P. 24. — The settlement of Roberval at Quebec was a disastrous failure. It is said that the King, in great need of Roberval, sent Cartier to bring him home. It is said, too, that, in after years, the Viceroy essayed to repossess himself of his transatlantic domain, and lost his life in the attempt. Thevet, on the other hand, with ample means of learning the truth, affirms that Roberval was slain at night, near the Church of the Innocents, in the heart of Paris. — Parkman, Pioneers of France.

EUDORA.

I.

Like a white blossom in a shady place,
    Upon her couch the pure Eudora lay,
Lovely in death ; and on her comely face,—
    So soon to make acquaintance with the clay,—
    Fell faint the languid light of evening gray,
Flecked with the pea-blooms at the window case.

II.

Deep sobbings echoed in the outer hall,
    And all things in the chamber seemed to mourn ;—
The pictures, which she loved, along the wall,
    The cherubs on the frescoed ceiling, lorn,
    Looked downward on the face so wan and worn,
And sad each wavy curtain's foamy fall.

III.

Born with the last, the long laborious sigh,
   Her soul, expanding upward, wondrous fair,
Lingered regretful, loath to seek the sky,
    Loath to forsake its sister-semblance there ;
    And, hovering in the chamber's dusky air,
Gazed on its blank abode with piteous eye.

IV.

There, too, glad-winged, impatient to depart,—
   Betwixt the fragrant window and the maid,—
The Angel-Guardian of her gentle heart,
    And now the escort of her trembling shade,
    Pointed to where the day-beams never fade,
Pointed their path on the celestial chart.

V.

Then spoke Eudora's Soul : " My comely shell,
   Bleached with a silent grief which we alone,
Which only thou and I have known too well,
    In cities and in solitudes have known,—
    Poor pallid tenement ! no more my own,
I grieve, and yet rejoice to say farewell !

VI.

" Rejoice that all thine agony is past,
  That never more on thee, my down-blown tent,
Will beat wild sorrow's suffocating blast ;—   [spent,
  And grieve that thou, with whom some years I've
  Albeit in latter days with discontent,
Must now into the nether night be cast.

VII.

" Once thou wert happy ; cheery nights and days
  Chasing each other o'er a flowery plain,
Like fairy lovers ; all thy modest ways
  Fell on fond hearts as falls the summer rain
  On heat-rived earth, on thirsty fields of grain,
And thine the golden harvest of their praise.

VIII.

" Half woman grown, half lost in reverie,
  Love's marvel came, and I, thine inner life,
Was calm and tempest-tossed alternately ;
  For though my fluttering heart with joy was rife,
  Some premonition of impending strife
Flitted betwixt us and futurity.

6

IX.

" The woods our secret knew; their quivering lips
     Uttered it audibly; the conscious flowers
Blushed as we passed them to their throbbing tips,
     And all the blissful warblers of green bowers
     Told it each morning to the waking hours ;—
Old ocean knew it, and the queenly ships.

X.

" O dream of dreams, too exquisite to stay !
     In which I sailed as in a rosy-cloud
That floats around the heavens a summer's day,
     And when at eve the drowsy woods are bowed,
     Responsive to the wind that calls aloud,
Is rent in fragments and dissolves away.

XI.

" So fled my dream when fled the vital spark
     Of loved Lysander ; Oh I his peerless eyes
Held all the light that piloted my bark,
     All the warm sunshine of entrancing skies.—
     ' Cold on the battle-field the hero lies,'
So sang the bards, and all the world grew dark ! "

XII.

At this her tender yearnings, all unplumed,
   Fluttered and faltered into silent awe,
And gasping pause ; two gleamy drops illumed
   Her incorporeal features, and the thaw
   Of frozen love·throbs, true to mercy's law,
Gave solace, and her heart-tale she resumed.—

XIII.

" A foreign despot dared invade our coast,
   And brave Lysander sped to meet the foe ;
His was the voice that led the patriot host,
   And his the arm that laid the tyrant low ;
   Thine own fond lips, Eudora, bade him go,
For love of country was thy girlish boast.

XIV.

" With triumph crowned our gallant warrior fell !
   And other suitors sought to win thy hand,
And kindred strove to break the evil spell,
   And deemed that travel in a distant land,—
   The Orient's classic vales and mountains grand,—
Might calm thy secret sorrow's turbid swell.

XV.

" In vain the Alps arose, in vain we gazed
    Up the sheer heights where climbed Napoleon's host,
And saw the towering peaks where crashed and blazed
    The war of storms that pleased Childe Harold most,
    Where now with Jura sits his gloomy ghost,
Above the world he loathed sublimely raised.

XVI.

" Nor Como's lovely lake, nor Arno's stream,
    Nor wonders of the Adriatic shore,
Nor those immortal cities which redeem
    From time and death a venerated lore,
    Whose spell the world confesses evermore,
Could shake the winter torpor of our dream.

XVII.

" O how my supplications eve and morn,
    Wrestled for him ! how frantic my appeal !—
And when he was not, I, a thing forlorn !
    Waylaid and robbed of hope, did cease to kneel,
    For Heaven no balsam had my hurt to heal,
And oft I wished that thou hadst ne'er been born."

XVIII.

The Spirit ceased, her humid eyes still bent
   On the prone form to which she fain would cleave;
Then thus the Angel: " Weak is thy lament!
   The joys of earth but sparkle to deceive,—
   And know you not that he for whom you grieve
Awaits our coming in the firmament?

XIX.

" Dear to the people dwelling in the skies
   Is he who for his country copes with death,
And, vanquished or victorious, nobly dies;
   The air that gives and takes his latest breath
   Is thence inhaled by souls of feeble faith,
And freedom flashes from their lifted eyes.

XX.

" Come! dear Eudora, while the waning light
   Burns on the lakes and on the mountain tops;
My arm shall aid thee in thy upward flight:—
   Soon shall we pass beyond those shining drops,
   Where utmost telescopic vision stops,
The limit of a Herschel's baffled sight.

XXI.

" See! chaste Andromeda unbinds her hair
   For us to tread upon ; we need not fear
Proud Leo wakeful in his azure lair,
    Nor Taurus' rampant horns and brow severe,
    Nor all the glittering terrors that appear
In Ursa's stormy mouth and hungry glare.

XXII.

"Come! every star now beckons us to come,
   O timid sister ! spread thy budded wings.
Dost thou not hear the sanctifying hum
    Of airy voices? precious whisperings ?
    List ! on the verge of heaven a seraph sings :—
'Come home, come hither, weary wanderers, come!'"

XXIII.

No more she spoke, but tremulous, amazed,
   With hands upon her panting bosom crost,
Far, far away abstractedly she gazed,
    As if in beatific vision lost,—
    As one just freed from earth's sepulchral frost,
And suddenly to 'wildering glories raised.

XXIV.

Only an instant thus, for now her Ward
   Became transfigured, robed in awful light;
Too beautiful for mortal man's regard;   [bright,
   And swift through cloudy rifts, with moonbeans
   These two immortals winged their starry flight,
Their home revealed, the golden gates unbarred.

88

THE VOICE OF THE AGES.

The years roll on, and with them roll
The burden of the human soul,
    The ache and pain
    Of heart and brain,
That hear far off a solemn night-bell toll.

List ! ringing clear, another sound
Reverberates the world around.
    The rapt Soul listens ;
    A tear-drop glistens
Down her pale cheek and trickles to the ground :—

A tear of joy, for she hath heard
The promise of the ancient Word
    Over the dark
    Prevailing : hark !
" All thy hopes, wan Soul, now sere and blurred,

Shall surely yet rebud and bloom ;
Discard thy self-spun robe of gloom,
    Awake ! arise !
    More just and wise,
Thy failing lamp with higher life relume.

The prophecy of ages past
Shall be fulfilled at last ;—
    Lo ! man shall rise
    With fadeless glory in his eyes,
His knowledge clarified, illumed and vast.

Thou wert of old, thou art, shalt be,
A thing unbound and ever free
    To work, and will,—
    A throb, a thrill,—
A joyous breath of immortality."

THE WOODLAND WALK.

Through the murk of the night, thou rememberest well,
　　The year and the month and the day of the week,
When we slipped away from that great hotel,
To escape the Babel of tongues that fell,
With wearisome sameness of sound and swell,
　　On ears that had wiser employ to seek.
The night was as calm as a child's first prayer,
　　And we did not venture one word to speak
Till we entered the path of the cool green wood,
And felt in our whispering hearts it was good,
　　For thee and me to be there.

Thy hand on my arm, we held our way
　　Till we came to the mountain lake,
　　The dear little woodland lake,
Where together we sat on its margin gray,
And queried on all they meant to say,

The batrachian people that round it spake ;—
And the peace of the skies, with stars o'erstrown,
Passed into our souls, my life ! my own !
    And I loved the universe more for thy sake.

Gladly we watched the full-orbéd moon
    Rising behind the shimmering trees,
Till she kissed their slumbering brows, when soon
In a silvery sea they sank in swoon.
    When over them ran a tremulous breeze,—
While they dreamt of joy and murmured their love
To the Lady who laughed at their worship above,—
    Making a mimic noon.

Down over the rim of the forest she looked,
    So chaste her beauty, all evil things,
    With or without or feet or wings,
In the might of her purity felt rebuked.—
She looked in her mirror, the lake, to behold
    Her image once more :—
    " It was lovely of yore,
And cannot grow charmless, cannot grow old,
No wrinkle the malice of years hath wrought
    On that envied brow, which is fair to-night

As when the first pair of true lovers sought
　My friendly smiles to aid their flight,
And hallow the vows their twin-hearts taught.

This to her image the chaste moon said ;—
　And such, my beloved, is thy face to me,
(Nay, do not shake that skeptical head,)
Ever as fair, ever as young,
As when first thy beauty inspired my tongue
　To pray the Fates that our names might be
Together engraved, and the tablet hung
　On the love-lit walls of eternity.

Athwart the white tablet if shadows are cast,
　As clouds the face of the moon perplex,
It is wiser to think they will not last,
However prolonged, and cold, and vast,
　Shadow and cloud will cease to vex.

These we will strive to forget, but not
　Our woodland walk on that July night,
When the craze of the world was quite forgot,
And heaven came down to the arbored spot,
　Where we bathed in Dian's crystal light.

The happy musicians around the lake,
Who kept all the infant echoes awake,
The bull-frogs bellow, the tree-toads trill,
The plaintive cry of the whip-poor-will,
And the hawk's alarm—I hear them still.

One hour of rest in the forest shade,
Where delicate mosses on rocks are laid,
　　And violets peep from under a stone,
Is a blissful exchange for the city's parade,
Its prodigal shows and masquerade,
　　Where mammon is king, and rest there is none.

Better than all the philosophy taught
By sages famed in the realm of thought ;—
Truer than sermons, wiser than books,
And honester far than the solemnest looks
Of parson or priest, was the ancient lore
That back from the woods in our hearts we bore,
The woods, and the lake and the lisping brooks,
To a world that is weary, yet rests nevermore.

STREET WAIF.

I.

From morn till noon, from noon till night,
Pacing the sidewalk, always in sight,
Who has not seen the mysterious wight?
    Is he man or ghost?
    Is he crazed or lost?
Does he walk with the fiends or the spirits of light?

II.

Answer, ye flagstones that echo his tread;—
Answer, ye cold winds that buffet his head;—
Tell us, ye clouds, that with pinions outspread
    Smite him with fire,
    And mock at his ire,
Shuns he the living for love of the dead?

Through the long lapse of the changing year
His crumbling garments unchanged appear,
The old drab coat, and the thing so queer
    Stuck to his pate !
    All out of date,
Tempting the urchins to point and jeer.—
    "*Poor waif !*"

III.

Poor waif !—'tis the murmur of angels who grieve ;
'Tis a voice from the clouds which my soul must
    receive.
Tell me the secret whose whispers bereave
    His eyelids of joy ;
    Preserve or destroy,
Crush him in mercy, or grant a reprieve.

IV.

Has he been guilty of some dark deed?
Surely no crime in that brow could breed !
So lofty, so mild in its terrible need ?
    Has he betrayed
    An innocent maid ?
Or plundered the poor to surfeit his greed ?

V.

Has he, for sake of a crumb and a sip,
With loyalty's cry evermore on his lip,
Counselled the use of a merciless whip
    When failure brought blame
    On the Patriot's name,
And tyrants their hot-sided beagles let slip?

VI.

Has he been cruel to nearest of kin?
The mother who loved him, and pleaded to win
Her prodigal back from the desert of sin?
    Has he struck in base ire
    The cheek of his sire?
Then plunge him in Acheron up to the chin.—
    " Poor waif !"

VII.

That tender refrain which the angels repeat,
The angels who hover o'er alley and street,
Let me interpret its sound as is meet.
    'Tis a pitiful cry !
    'Tis the sob of the sky !—
Is he the victim of woman's deceit?

VIII.

O, ye invisible shapes of the air—
Ye watchers that wait upon heaven—declare,
Sees he naught else but a face that is fair?

    Murmur again
    The tender refrain,

If that and that only, hath wrought his despair.—
    " *Poor waif!* "

IX.

Then have I wronged him! and grieve at his fate
But love's load of sorrow no love can abate,
Naming, still naming her, early and late.

    A dim dream of bliss,
    The soft light of a kiss,

Only may enter through memory's gate.

X.

Within, what a ruin! arch, column and cope,
The palace of wisdom, ambition, and hope,
All broken and blasted! what spectres now grope

    Through the blue charnel gloom
    Of each desolate room!   [mope.—

Blind, shrivelled and maimed, they but mumble and
    " *Poor waif!* "

7

XI.

Now am I certain that beauty's false art,
A maid's broken promise hath broken his heart
No other evil such look could impart
      To manhood's fair brow ;
      Only speak of her now,
And mark how the eye-drowning sorrow will start

XII.

Wild-eyed, but erect as a soldier-king,
Through the *Rue St. Jacques*, with a tireless swing,
Onward he strides ; let the fire-bells ring,
      And their terror outpour,
      While the red flames roar,
Nothing cares he for the summons they fling.

XIII.

And why should he care? why linger, or start?
The fierce-hissing tongues that the fire-fiends dart
From window and roof, from the square to the mart,
      Are harmless and mild,
      As the laugh of a child,
Compared to the tempest of flame in his heart.

XIV.

Why care ? when the thousands who sweep through
    the city,
The judge with black cap, and the maid with her
    ditty,
Bestow on love's ruin no question of pity.
      The crowds that he meets
      On the merciless streets
Only smite him anew with some word that is witty.

XV.

Kind ghosts, whose compassionate voices I hear
High up in the air, come hither, come near !
Close down his eyelids and fashion his bier ;
      O let him pass
      Under flower and grass !
Men are too busy to grant him a tear.

XVI.

Good angels ! stoop earthward and bear him away
Out of the city's tumultuous fray ;
Tenderly kiss his parched lips, and then lay
      His body to rest
      On the mountain's lone breast,
Where shadows and sunbeams in happiness play !

THE SONG OF A GLORIFIED SPIRIT

A youth knelt down by a new made grave
    Unseen by the world, and wept ;—
A sister whose beauty no love could save
    Beneath in the darkness slept.

'Twas a calm, sweet eve, and on hill and plain
    The summer had lavished her dower ;
But the full sad heart of the youth could gain
    No solace from sun or flower.

The big warm tears he wiped from his cheek,
    As he said with a struggling faith,
" O God, if I could but hear her speak !—
    My sister ! now thine, O death ! "

In silence and sorrow he lingered long,
   And just as he rose to depart,
In the heavens was warbled this saintly song,
   Which fell like a balm on his heart :

" Beautiful are my walks in the sky,
             Beautiful, beautiful !
Here the amaranths never die,
Here the sweet winds murmur and sigh,
             Beautiful, beautiful !

" Joyfully glide my golden hours,
             Joyfully, joyfully !
Here the leaves of the hyacinth flowers
Whisper around my love-lit bowers :
             Joyfully, joyfully !

" Lovingly smile my comrades here,
             Lovingly, lovingly !
All the bright shapes of this blissful sphere
Tell how that each unto each is dear,
             Lovingly, lovingly !

"Merciful is my Father, my all,

        Merciful, merciful !

Here the white-cheeked lilies, so tall,

Sing in their place by the jasper wall :

        Merciful, merciful !

NOTE.—The origin of this lyric may possibly be of interest. A young friend had lost an only sister and, in an outburst of passionate sorrow, had exclaimed " O God if I could hear her speak." Brooding over his sorrow, I retired to rest one evening and without attempting to embody my sympathy in words, I fell into a quiet slumber which lasted until day light. On waking, I had a vivid recollection of having seen in dream the youth kneeling by his sister's grave and of having heard the words of his sister's spirit chanted from the empyrean with inexpressible sweetness as if responding to his yearning exclamation. The words I heard in my dream I wrote down immediately lest their exactness and coherency might be lost. I was not at that time aware that Kubla Khan originated in a somewhat similar manner. As the occurrence, if standing alone, might seem difficult to believe, I refer to Coleridge's poem merely to justify in some degree the publication of such a freak of the imagination.

BOUND TO THE WHEEL.

I.

Must I grind in this prison for ever ?
　No respite from morn till night ;
Shall I never again, oh, never !
　Commune with the spirits of light
That dwell by the crystalline river
　Which flows by the Sibylline height ?—
　Which sings near the Sibylline height ?

II.

I sigh for that region romantic,
　Far away from the turmoil and strife
Of cities that render men frantic
　In a desperate struggle for life ;
For 'tis here that ambition gigantic
　Cuts into the heart like a knife,—
　Lies cold on the heart like a knife.

III.

There Beauty sits thronéd in glory,
  The bards kiss her brow and adore,
Then tell to the world the sweet story
  That millions repeat evermore ;
The youth and the patriarch hoary
  Bend over the musical lore,—
  Never tire of the mystical lore.

IV.

It is there the perpetual graces,
  Inhabiting bowers of bliss,
Give welcome to wearisome faces
  That 'scape from a region like this,
A world in whose gaudiest places
  The serpent is sure to hiss,—
  The black-crested serpent will hiss.

V.

I know now the fate of Ixion
  As I never could know it before ;
And under the eyes of Orion,—

Storm-bound on a desolate shore,—
Or under the paws of the Lion,
   I sigh for the sorrows he bore ;—
   I know, too, what Sisyphus bore.

VI.

Must I grind in this dungeon for ever!
   Will the day of release never dawn?
Come, spirits of light, and deliver
   My soul which I ventured to pawn ;
Oh, bear her away to the river
   That flows by the Sibylline lawn,—
   The sylph-haunted Sibylline lawn.

THE APPLE WOMAN.

(*From life.*)

I.

She often comes, a not unwelcome guest,
   With her old face set in a marble smile,
And bonnet ribbonless—it is her best,—
   And little cloak—and blesses you the while,
   And cracks her joke, ambitious to beguile
      Your heart to something human,
Then sets her basket down—a little rest !
     The Apple Woman.

II.

Her stock in trade that basket doth contain;
   It is her wholesale and her retail store,

Her goods and chattels,—all that doth pertain
　To her estate, a daughter of the Poor;
　O ye who tread upon a velvet floor,
　　　　Whose walls rich lights illumine,
Wound not, with word or look of high disdain,
　　　　The Apple Woman.

III.

She is thy sister, jewelled Lady Clare,
　"My sister! fling this insult in my face?"
How dare you then, when in the house of prayer,
　Utter, Our Father? difference of place
　Nulls not the consanguinity of race,
　　　　And every creature human
Is kin to that poor mother, shivering there,
　　　　The Apple Woman.

IV.

She sits upon the side-walk in the cold,
　And with her scraggy hand, hard, shrunk and blue,
And corded with the cordage of the old,
　She reaches forth a *fameuse*, sir, to you,

And begs her ladyship will take one, too,
                And if you are a true man
Your pence will out; she never thinks of *gold*,
                The Apple Woman.

v.

She tells me—and I know she tells me true,
    "My good man,—God be kind!—had long been
        sick,
And one cold morning when the snow-storm blew,
    He said, dear Bess, it grieves me to the quick
    To see you venture out,—give me my stick,
                I'll come to you at gloamin,'
And bide you home,"—she paused, the rest I knew.—
                Poor Apple Woman!

vi.

Behold her then, a type of all that's good,
    Honest in poverty, in suffering kind;
And large must be that love which strains for food,
    Through wind and rain, through frost and snows
        that blind,

For a sick burden that is left behind ;
Call her but common ;
God's commonest things are little understood,
Poor Apple Woman !

VII.

Two April weeks I missed her, only two,
Missed her upon the sidewalk, everywhere,
And when again she chanced to cross my view,
The marble smile was changed, it still was there,
But darkly veined, an emblem of despair ;
A God-knit union
Grim death had struck, whose dark shock shivered
through
The Apple Woman.

VIII.

A widow now, she tells the bitter tale,
Tells how she sat within their little room
In yon dark alley, till she saw him fail,
Sat all alone through night's oppressive gloom,
Sat by her Joe, as in a desert tomb,

No candle to illumine
His cold dead face ! God only heard her wail.—
Poor Apple Woman.

IX.

Now, when you meet her of the basket-store,
   Her of the little cloak and bonnet bare,
Reach forth a friendly hand, and something more,
   When your portmonnaie has a coin to spare.
   Dear are the hopes that mitigate thy care,
      Dear the unbought communion
Whose tall vine reaches to the golden shore.—
      Poor Apple Woman !

ON MOUNT ROYAL.

I.

They sat in the woods together,
  On the mountain's tranquil height,
And spoke of the Autumn weather,
  Of the purplish-golden light
That played on the distant river,
  And robed the mountains afar
In a robe more rich than ever
  Was worn by Caliph or Czar.

II.

The wine of the beauty around them
  They drank till the sun hung low,
Till the scene like a spell had bound them;
  For the forest was all aglow

With the countless tints that follow
  Spent Summer's retiring tread,
When freely on height and hollow
  All beautiful colours are shed.

III.

All hues that the rainbow showeth,
  All opulent dyes that flush
The western sky when goeth
  The Lord of Day, and the blush
Of river and lake and ocean
  Betrays that his last caress
Their life-blood keeps in motion
  Till he cometh again to bless.

IV.

No valley of famed Cashmere
  Such exquisite tints puts on
As the woods that crown the year,
  When hot-footed Summer is gone
When every tree is a flower,
  Gigantic, superbly aflame

With ruby and scarlet,—a dower
Of beauty no tongue can name.

V.

They sat and communed together ;
She spoke of this dream of life,
And quietly questioned whether
'Tis worth all the sorrow and strife
That burden the hearts of many,
That tangle the steps cf all ;
For truly there is not any
Who 'scapeth the serpent's thrall.

VI.

He said : "Such a thought but troubles
The good that in life we find,
Distorts fair truth, and doubles
The anguish that clouds the mind.
Surely, this cirque of beauty,
And that blue heaven above,
Make love of life a duty,
And life a thing to love."

8

VII.

She said : " The winter cometh ;
   These splendors will cease to be,
Like the joy in the heart that hummeth
   An hour for you and me,
Then suddenly sinks to ashes,
   So perish all beautiful things ;
So love for an instant flashes,
   Then folds his languid wings."

VIII.

" Ah ! now I suspect you dissemble,"
   He presently made reply ;
" You need not fear or tremble,
   For surely you and I
Have faith in love's endurance
   And know that beauty abides
For souls that in blest assurance
   Discern where it haply hides."

IX.

In silent and solemn abstraction
   She gazed on the pictured trees,

Through which a pale reflection
    Of light and a friendly breeze
Shimmered and sighed so kindly,—
    She dreamily said: " Maybe
Too coldly, perchance too blindly,
    I've judged of this world—and thee !"

X.

A tear in her bright eye glistened,
    The soft breeze wafted her hair
Adrift on his face, when she listened
    As if to a voice in the air;
But neither by word nor token
    Behooves it the world to know
How the chain of her doubt was broken,
    Whilst the sun in the West hung low.

XI.

The low wind hastened to utter
    A message of joyful sound;
Like flakes of fire a-flutter
    Some red leaves fell to the ground;
A chorus of bells in the city

Rose mournfully mellow and clear,
Like voices of infinite pity
For lives that were saddened and sere.

XII.

They rose and descended the mountain,
So happy and hallowed in thought,
Charmed nature to them was a fountain
Of tender emotion that wrought
A longing for nobler endeavour
To make life to others a boon
As peaceful and blessed forever
As their dream of that afternoon.

MAIDEN LONGINGS.

Sitting, thinking, all alone,
Listening to the beetle's drone,
And the night-hawk's monotone ;
Sitting, sighing, thus alone,
     How my heart is longing !

Yet I could not tell you why
Tears will gather in my eye
When the night-winds tread the sky ;
No, I could not answer why,
     Or for what, I'm longing.

Solemn as the rapid's roar,
Sounding on my native shore,
Is my heart's dream evermore ;
Oh ! for some old wizard's lore
     To ease this weary longing.

Vague the cause that moves me so;—
Is it love? Ah no! no! no!!
It can't be love that shakes me so,
When the stars in regal show
      Around their Queen are thronging.

ASPIRATION.

I.

" What Cyclopean force is this I feel,
  Heaving the central fires within my heart?
While full-orbed splendors round my spirit wheel,
  And, gazing into vacant space, I start,
  For seems a fair hand beckons me apart.
            Oh ! I will try,
            Before I die,
To find a voice this mystery to reveal.

II.

" Why do I seem to sit upon a cloud,
  Wearing the crimson mantle of the sun,
Delighted when the wind-god shrieks aloud,
  And raptured when the midnight thunder-gun
  Tells where the nimble-footed lightnings run ?
            Shall I not try
            Ere age draw nigh
Some world-enticing poem to unshroud ?

III.

" Why do the by-gone years, with accents cold,
     Call to me through the darkness from their grave,
Till thinking on their dowry, tears are rolled
     Down my wan cheeks?   I think of all they gave,
     And all they stole from me, their fool and slave.
               Earnestly I,
               Henceforth will try
To sublimate my life to purest gold.

IV.

" And often while I dally with the Night,
     Running my fingers through her raven hair,
There floats up to my shocked and tearful sight
     An angel's face, transformed with pain and care
     O, maiden ! long beloved, I see you there,
               But you and I
               May never try
To braid our love into a zone of light.

V.

" The organ of the Universe is played
     By bards who strike the keys with master sweep,

Upon its music-waves I float, afraid,
    Yet joyous, doubtful if to smile or weep,
    And haunted by its sea of sound in sleep,
        I wake to try
        A purpose high—
To earn the poet's crown before I fade.

VI.

" O, Heaven ! while my spirit gladly sings,
    Shape her vague tremblings to some useful end,
And purify my strange imaginings,
    That when the better years which hither tend,
    Pass on, I may be called Man's poet-friend,
        Thus will I try,
        Before I die
To shake the earth-dregs from my soaring wings."

VII.

So sang a poet by the harping sea,
    And thick as white shells strewn upon the beach,
Fancies came thronging to him, wild and free,
    And bade him limn their airy forms in speech :
    But still he only sang with aimless reach,

ASPIRATION.

> " All things do cry
> Pilgrim, try !
> Thrill the tame world with sun-lit poesy."

VIII.

Years rolled away, and by the sea-licked shore
　　The moonbeams quivered on a lonely mound ;
The pilgrim-poet's turbulence was o'er,
　　And that secluded spot was holy ground ;
　　For he with songs of wondrous love had crowned
　　　　Insulted Right ;
　　　　And pure and bright
His verse illumed the sorrows of the poor.

IX.

He left behind him, though he knew it not,
　　A trail of glory on the world's highway,
And loving fingers now denote the spot
　　Where he was wont to build the witching lay,
　　And champions of mind, admiring, say,
　　　　" Grandly he tried,
　　　　Before he died,
To teach dull earth the majesty of thought."

THE HAWK AND THE SPARROW.

I.

To-day, upon the public square,
I saw a hawk in fury tear
A sparrow : hapless little thing,
The tyrant rent it wing from wing
And limb from limb, and on the snow
Its life-drops made a crimson glow.

II.

I drove the feathered fiend away,
And gathered up the mangled prey ;
And pondering o'er the fragments red,
I thought of what is writ and said :
" *The Omnipresent Lord of all*
Has knowledge of a sparrow's fall."

III.

I thought,—if the omnific Lord
Commiserates a dying bird,
If all things act by his design,
And swerve not from his plumb and line,
Why did he arm with murderous beak
That hawk to slay a thing so weak
And harmless as our little friend?

IV.

No more the maple twig will bend
Beneath his feet; his life's swift end
One faithful mourner, one at least,—
His sexton now and reverent priest,—
Deplores; does He who gave him life,
And walled him round with tragic strife,
Feel equal pity?   Why, O why
This outrage under all His sky?

V.

Is He too weak the weak to save?
To His own laws is He a slave?
If not, then wherefore were the laws

Permitted with such fatal flaws?
Surely the heavy curse that fell
On Adam, sloping down to hell,
Cannot in justice overtake
Aught less than human, save the snake?

VI.

A soft voice answered, soft and still:
"This mystery of earthly ill
'Tis well to probe, 'tis well to seek
All knowledge, and to freely speak,
Since love of truth thy soul impels,
And love of goodness in thee dwells.
Well, too, the sympathetic tear
Bestowed upon the sparrow here;
But scarcely was it well to balk,
Or rudely blame the famished hawk.

VII.

" High knowledge is not ready-made,
And darker grows the mental shade,
If you pursue your curious quest;
Why with the hawk and sparrow rest?

How many of thy boastful race
Would spare the hawk in any case—
Would spare or pity, though his need
Your lordly sportsman could not plead.
Moreover this poor bird whose doom
Has touched thy feeling heart with gloom,
No tender scruple ever made
With creatures of an humbler grade,
So, puzzling o'er these knots of fate,
Life's riddle grows more intricate.

VIII.

" Who seeks will rarely fail to find
The thing to which he's most inclined.
If thorns instead of roses suit,—
If leaves instead of luscious fruit,—
If turbid waters more than clear,—
If doleful sounds in place of cheer,—
Those will respect the cynic's right,
While *these* elude his senses quite.

IX.

" Doubt if thou wilt, but reverently,

And heed not what the owls may say,
Who from their gloomy perch give out
That sin is foster-child of Doubt.
Doubt is the silent needful night,
The womb of intellectual might;
But who can wisely choose to dwell
Forever in that darksome shell?

X.

" The fearless soul emerging thence
Feels something of omnipotence ;—
Upon the mountain-tops his feet
Will tread in joy, and gladly beat
The golden shores of summer seas ;
And he will hear in every breeze
Divinest music ; even the storm
That bends the proud oak's stubborn form,
And howls athwart the naked land,
Will bring to him an utterance grand,
Engendering noble thoughts, and power
To serve him in some trying hour.

XI.

" Revere fair Nature's balanced laws,

Nor rashly deem them framed with flaws;
The discord which thou seem'st to find
In them is part of thine own mind.
Put that in tune, and, for the sake
Of darkened faces, strive to make
The world more happy; do this thing,
And thy despondent muse shall wring
Sweet nectar out of weed and cloud."

XII.

Silent, though unconvinced, I bowed
My head abashed; with firmer trust,
And higher faith, I shook the dust
Of utter doubt from reason's plume;
And through small openings in the gloom
I half discerned a meaning new
In that which seemed before untrue:
The ever-present Lord of all
Compassionates a sparrow's fall.

CELESTINE.

I.

I must not look on you nor think of you,—
　　Must seek close kinship with forgetfulness;
Such looks as thine but make a strong man rue
　　That ever in his heart's devout excess
The shadow of thy soul he did pursue
　　Through many a golden hour for one caress;
　　　　'Twas but a noontide dream,
　　　　A phantom fire, a gleam
Of heaven wasted in a wilderness.

II.

I wake and wonder at the vision gone,
　　Sweet music borne upon a winter blast,
A beauty filched from sunset and the dawn,
　　A marvel too ethereal to last;
And now a heavy sadness falls upon

9

My spirit and the world, both overcast
      With thunderstorm and gloom,
      In which there is no room
For any ray of the enchanted past.

III.

I chide the fond delirium of my brow,
   And only pray that you forgive, forget
The homage of a man who doth avow
   His folly with a penitent's regret ;
Such adoration even the gods allow,
   For thou art as a star divinely set
         In heaven's perfect blue,
         I can but sigh for you
In lonely ways with night dews chilled and wet.

TO A YOUNG LADY.

When Morn, in spring glory,
　Salutes the dull earth,
How sweet is her story
　Of music and mirth.

The happy leaves glisten
　And tremble around,
The young blossoms listen
　With joy to the sound.

They tell by their blushes,
　Their soft breathing proves,
That night's dewy hushes
　Promoted their loves.

The murmur of grasses,
　The singing of birds,
In sweetness surpasses
　The compass of words.

TO A YOUNG LADY.

Far away on the mountain
    The mist is on fire,
And the joy of the fountain
    Can soar up no higher.

A tremor of gladness
    Pervadeth the air,
And no touch of sadness
    Can rest anywhere.

We cease to be mortal
    In moments like this,
And enter the portal
    Of absolute bliss.

At noon, and at even,
    We think of the morn,
In the midst of whose heaven
    Such beauty is born.

'Tis thus I shall cherish
    Till life's gloaming end,
And never let perish
    The face of a friend.

Then come, gentle maiden,
And dwell with the few
That in my soul's Aidenn
I know to be true ;—

Some distant, some sleeping
The sleep of the just,
Are here in the keeping
Of memory's trust.

With these let thy spirit
Abide in its place,
So shall I inherit
New goodness and grace.

BETRAYED.

These verses embody the last thoughts recorded in the Journal of a young lady of a village on the banks of the St. Lawrence, who was found dead in her chamber on a bright June morning of 186—, and was supposed to have committed suicide during the night.

Henceforth a wanderer,
　　Hie thee, my soul,
Over life's frozen waste,
　　Haste to thy goal.

O never again
　　Shall the down of sweet rest
Pillow thy weariness,
　　Spirit unblest !

No fair land of promise
　　Thy vision can reach ;
No sunshine, no music,
　　No glory of speech.

Regrets and reproaches
　　Are idle and weak,
And the insult of pity
　　Brings shame to the cheek.

Farewell, ruined world !—
　　In the depth of star spaces
There may be sweet slumber,
　　And love-beaming faces.

There must be some spot
　　In this Universe wide,
Where a poor wounded dovelet
　　May haste to and hide.

The raven has flown
　　To his perch through the gloom,
And the death-watch is calling
　　His mate in my room.

The wail of the winds,
　　And the rapid's loud roar,
Have a weirdness and terror
　　Felt never before.

BETRAYED.

A gray mist has settled
  On land and on sea,
And night-dews are falling,
  My spirit, on thee !

When day-light is gone,
  And the glimmer of stars,
Like a ghost at the casement,
  Looks in through the bars,

It is time to disrobe,
  And to kneel down and weep,
To forgive and forget,—
  It is time now to sleep !

EPITHALAMIUM.

Written in honour of the nuptials of two young friends.
(1882.)

Moonlight Chant of Fairies, crowned with maple leaves.

Scene :—Mount Royal, Canada.

I.

Speed, thou fiery monster, speed,
Let thy chariot wheels take heed
    That they out-strip flight of beagle,
Till our Benedict they've borne
To his little maiden, lorn,
    In the Land where screams the Eagle.

Linger, star of evening, linger,
Like the gem upon her finger,
    While she sits, her love-notes humming,
At her casement, watching, waiting—
With her busy heart debating—
    For the magic of his coming.

II.

The Goblin of Celibacy chagrined.

Scene :—On the border.

Oh—ho ! they have escaped my grip ;
How stupid I, to let them slip !
   The fools ! to lose their free estate !
These rash and idiotic pranks,
These sly desertions from my ranks
   Have multiplied so fast of late
That few remain, save priests and nuns,
And some fastidious elder sons
   To honour still the heavenly call,
And piously their loves resign,
Obedient to the word divine,
   The gospel preached by good St. Paul.

III.

Hymenæus, exultant.

Scene :—Newark, N. J.

Welcome hither, happy pair ;
All my bounties freely share,

Welcome to my honoured guild,
Founded in the days of old,
Ere the human heart grew cold,
  Ere its native warmth was chilled
By mistaken sense of duty ;—
By sacrifice of youth and beauty
To Plutus, with his lure of gold.
Fear not any churlish cry ;
To the Goblin bid good-bye ;
Enter, children, bravely enter
To my circle's shining centre,
    Clasping hands ;
Stronger far than iron bands
Be your love, and hope and trust ;
Equal freedom, fairest speech,
Give I lavishly to each.
See that neither moth nor rust,
Nor cobweb, nor insidious dust
Of cold neglect, e'er dim the light
That lights you from my torch to-night.

By my crown, unfading, bright—
Sweet marjoram and dewy roses—
Emblem of the sovereign might

Which wedded love to hate opposes ;—
By this purple vest, symbolic
  Of the royal rank of marriage,
  Which the fiends alone disparage,
Mocking in their witless frolic ;—
By this mystic torch, whose glow
On your souls I now bestow ;—
By all these tokens joined, I swear
To have you in my constant care,
  But I warn you, neophytes,
Warn you ever to beware
How you guard the altar reared
  In my honour, ages gone :
    Subtle is the snake that bites ;
  Wintry days will come anon ;
  Evil must be fought, not feared ;
  No fiend can harm, no god subdue
  The soul that to itself is true.
  To virtue be your homage paid,
  And firmly hold the golden clue
  Of knowledge, whose imperial aid
  Is truly sought and found by few.
  These farewell words in memory keep,
  Or when you laugh or when you weep.

IV.

Salutation from the King of the Beavers.

Scene :—Canadian side of the border.

Happy couple, Bride and Groom,
In the flush of life's fresh bloom,
Welcome to the kindly home
Where we shape the wattled dome,
Cemented o'er with plastic clay,
Impervious to the water's play ;
Where, in moonlight's silver calm,
My faithful subjects build the dam ;
The land whose maple leaf conveys
A prophecy of sweetened days.
Our store of knowledge is but scant,
Our culture in the shell, I grant.
No prophet of our kith and kin
Have we to point the paths of sin ;
No learned Professor, beaver born,
Have we to rend in godly scorn
The sophistries our Darwins weave,
O'er which our pious pundits grieve.
I pray you, therefore, not impeach
The rudeness of our rustic speech,

But hear the fancies, none the less,
An honest beaver may express.

Your wisest men, the lords of thought,
Remote and near, have ever sought,
Instruction from the humblest things
That beat the air on filmy wings,
Or creep, or climb, or swim the sea :
Behold the little " busy bee ; "
Go to, thou sluggard, cursed with want,
And learn from the industrious ant.
" The early bird ; " the cooing dove,
Exemplar of the art of love.
A spider once, at climbing brave,
Fresh courage to a chieftain gave,
When, after many a sore defeat,
His hopes were all in full retreat ;
But noting how the insect fell
Time after time, and naught could quell
Its resolution, firm and fast,
And how it reached its mark at last,
No longer chilled with black despair,
His men he rallied, sword in air,
And ere another set of sun

His last great battle fought and won.
And then his tribe—a proper thing—
Made him, like me, their lawful king.
The nautilus, your sages own,
To all mankind have plainly shown
The art of how to sail the seas ;
Such creatures low in life as these
Have served to educate and guide ;
Meet glossary on human pride !
The several nations show their bent
By what their ruling minds invent
To signify the special merit
That each assumes, or doth inherit.
Their boastful banners proudly bear
The savage forms of earth and air,
And monstrous shapes in neither seen,
Things that were hatched in human spleen,
Creatures patched up from beast and bird,
Which to a beaver seems absurd.
Dragons and griffins, flying fierce,
With fiery tongues designed to pierce
All alien flesh, wherever found,
And claws to clinch the deadly wound.
The warlike Briton, while he cheers,

The lion's roar in fancy hears ;
The Yankee in his happiest dream
Is sure he hears the eagle scream.

These truths the higher truth explain
That dawned on Darwin's pregnant brain
Such deference paid to creatures low
Man's wiser instincts clearly show.
Unconsciously compelled to grant,—
By choosing for his common want,
As teachers, elephant and ant,
And other poor relations, in
Obedience to the law of kin,—
He owns his humble origin.

I know not if in any place,
Or any age, your lifted race
Its sense of equity hath shown
To one poor beast—we needs must own
Compact of kinship, bone of bone,
By making him an emblem fit
Of human wisdom, sense, and wit ;
A patient brother, void of blame,
I hesitate to name his name,

But—no offence—I dare not pass
Our worthy, long-eared friend, the ass.

Forgetful that your hunters slay
My people, and their bodies flay.
That human skins, puffed up with pride,
Strut forth in ours—no tongue to chide—
We're grateful for the honour given
To beaverhood, since nearer heaven
This great Dominion raised our name,
Emblazoned on the scroll of fame ;
A choice that to the world attests
The base on which its greatness rests,
Our one transcendent, special gift :—
Persistency of honest thrift.

  My sermon may appear to you
  But wind and chaff, however true ;
  Reject it if you will.—Adieu !

v.

Serenade of Fairies, crowned with ivy.

Scene :—A street in Montreal, West End.
Time :—November.

Welcome home, our Benedict !
  10

To duty never less than strict ;
 Welcome thrice thy comely Bride !
Spirit of the frozen north !
Come not from thy palace forth,
 Yet a little while abide :

Tarry till the waning moon
Mournful, goes, as if too soon
 Summoned from these lucent skies.
Twinkle, joyful, all ye stars !
Peeping through your silver bars,
 Rivalled by their laughing eyes.

Hallowed be their sweet repose
When those eyes in slumber close,
 When they listen, pleasure-haunted,
To the melody we pour
Down the chimney, through the door,
 Listen in their dreams, enchanted.

IN THE WOODS OF ST. LEON.

Let who will sing of cities grand,
    Give me the woods, the endless shade
    Of trees on which no man e'er laid
        A ruthless hand.

What peace, what blissful quietude
    The rustle of these polished leaves
    Around my dreamy spirit weaves
        In this green wood !

Why have I fretted so and striven
    In populous towns among my kind,
    Where men, who think they see, are blind
        And prate of heaven ?

Here in this forest breathing spice,
    And love-lorn odors, born of flowers
    That woo me to their secret bowers,
        Is paradise.

The droning of the humble-bee,
 The soughing of the wind that stirs
 These pine-tops and aspiring firs,
  Bring joy to me.

Stretched on this knoll of soft brown spines,
 Let me life's true elixir drink,
 Nor even tax myself to think,
  Till day declines.

THE LOVER'S DREAM.

Last night,
When all the world was still,—
All but the whip-poor-will,—
A vision bright
Beamed on my lonely sleep,
On eyes late used to weep,
And robed the world in light.

My dear !
I saw thee once again
All beautiful, as when
In moonlight clear
We vowed beside the lake,
No fiend should ever shake,
Our plighted love sincere.

THE LOVER'S DREAM.

She came
From forth an azure cloud,
And, like an angel, bowed
    Fond o'er my frame,
And with her heavenly look,
While I, with transport, shook,
    Breathed lovingly my name.

    A moan !
I woke, the vision fled,
And feverish on my bed
    Till daylight shone,
I turned, and wept, and turned,
While on my lips still burned
    The pressure of her own.

    O Death !
Whose harshness did not spare
A face and form so fair,
    Whoever saith
Thou art to all the wise
A blessing in disguise,
    Wastes only idle breath.

No more :—
Ah ! how that sound, *no more*,
Travels from shore to shore
      The wide world o'er ;—
No more shall she entwine
Her young heart's joy with mine,
      Save such as dreams restore.

      Ye dreams !
That do unveil the past,
And o'er our spirits cast
      Supernal gleams,
Do you deceive us quite,
Gray Wizards of the night ?
      Is all not what it seems ?

      The sage,
With philosophic look
The simple may rebuke
      From age to age,
And speculations deep
Of mind and matter, heap
      On his immortal page :—

His skill,
Majestic though it be,
And dearly loved by me,
Is weakness still ;
I would not cast away
The thought that spirits may
In true communion thrill.

O bright,
And beautiful ; again,
Again, come to me when
Sleep seals my sight ;
Come with those love-lit eyes,
Come with thy fragrant sighs,
Come, love, O come to-night.

THE HEROES OF VILLE–MARIE.

May, 1660.

I.

Tis a tale of those times that afflicted the West,
When the exiles of France found no moment of rest.
When the yell of the savage, the gleam of his knife,
Ever kept the lone settler on watch for his life.

II.

The doom is proclaimed! 'twas the Sachems that spoke,
And rising, the calumet fiercely they broke;
The war-dance is danced, and the war-song is sung
And the warriors full-painted, their weapons have slung.

III.

Each armed with his arquebuse, hatchet and knife,
How they hunger and thirst for the barbarous strife!

They have said it : *The Frenchmen shall sleep with the
   slain,*
Maid, matron and babe—not a soul shall remain /—

IV.

They have spoken—those braves of the Iroquois
   league,
Renowned for fierce courage and shrewdest intrigue,
Through the Ottawa forest like panthers they tread,
As if stepping already o'er pale-visaged dead.

V.

Young Daulac, defender of fair Ville-Marie,
Has pondered and prayed o'er the savage decree,
And a desperate purpose is stamped on his brow,
And no one can slacken his ultimate vow.

VI.

Will heaven not baffle the merciless threat ?
Can the gracious Madonna her children forget ?
If God only grant him his people to save,
Then welcome red tomahawks, welcome the grave !

VII.

But who will give heed to the patriot's word?
Who will venture to follow the flash of his sword?
They must stand to the last bleeding man by his side,
And quench with their life-drops the Iroquois' pride.

VIII.

There are some—oh, how few!—in the bloom of their
    years,
Who have listened and pledged him, and trampled
    their fears;
With hot hearts as brave as their sabres are keen,
They are mustered around him—his gallant *Sixteen*.

IX.

Kind Priest and sad Nuns their last blessing bestow,
And kindred are weeping, for well do they know
That never again, till they meet in the skies,
Will the faces so dear to them gladden their eyes.

X.

They are gone! they have wafted their final adieu,

And the cross on Mount Royal soon fades from their
    view ;
Now westward, now northward they paddle and plod—
Their trust in the piloting hand of their God !

XI.

In a ready redoubt, as by Providence meant,
They hastily fashion their evergreen tent.
And here in the forest, where Ottawa flows,
They prepare for the speedy descent of their foes.

XII.

Oh ! rest—weary soldiers, oh I sleep—while the stars
Are shining above you through leaf-fretted bars ;
But fail not to rouse with the glimmer of day,
For already the Mohawks have scented their prey.

XIII.

One last happy dream of the loved ones at home,—
One matinal prayer ere the cannibals come,—
One sigh for their sweethearts in young Ville-Marie,—
And a cheer for old France and her proud fleur-de-lis.

XIV.

The song of the bobolink welcomes the morn,
And scents that are sweetest, of wild flowers born,
And pine-lavished odors, are borne by the breeze
That kisses, at random, the newly-robed trees.

XV.

Full-crowned with proud antlers, the stag at the brink
Of the far-sounding rapid has halted to drink ;
He starts, blows a signal of danger and dread,
And his mate with her fawn seeking safety has fled.

XVI.

Hark ! near and still nearer, yell answers to yell,
All the forest seems peopled with spectres of hell !
Not a tree but now looks as if changed to a fiend,
Not a rock but behind it a demon is screened.

XVII.

" Thank God," Daulac said, " for this moment supreme,
The reply to my prayer,—vivid truth of my dream ;—
Now steady, all ready, my men,—let them dance
To the glory of Canada, glory of France."

XVIII.

From the loop-holed redoubt their first volley they
    pour,
And Mohawks and Sene cas sink in their gore ;
From musket, and huge musketoon, they have seen—
And heard—that our heroes count just *Seventeen.*

XIX.

And dire is the rage of the shame-smitten crew
When they find that the pale-faces number so few ;
Again and again comes the stormy attack,
And still the fierce pagans are forced to fall back.

XX.

Day and night, night and day, till the tenth set of
    sun (1)
No trophy the maddened assailants have won,
Though their fleet-footed runners have hurried from
    far
Half a thousand tried allies—hot whirlwinds of war.

XXI.

The leaves of past summers that cumber the ground

In pools of bright ruby and purple are drowned,
And, reckless of wounds, through the tempest of lead,
The discomfited Iroquois bear off their dead.

XXII.

Onondagas, Cayugas, Oneidas are there,
Some howling for vengeance, some wild with despair
Once again, with a hurricane rush and a shout,
Like a deluge of lightning they storm the redoubt.

XXIII.

They are hidden from death by their bison-hide
    shields, (2)
And long wooden bucklers,—the Palisade yields!
But brief is the daring—abrupt is the speech—
Of the foremost who boastingly enters the breach.

XXIV.

In a moment 'tis over! flash blending with flash,
As sword-blades and tomahawks bloodily clash;
" *Vive le Canada !*" Daulac exultantly cried,
Then with cross to his lips, like a martyr he died.

XXV.

The victors their victory purchased so dear,
To their cantons they fled, overmastered with fear,
And the grateful young Colony, saved from the knife
And merciless tomahawk, bloomed with fresh life.

XXVI.

Oh, never shall Canada coldly forget
Her heroes, whose heart-drops her virgin soil wet;
Their fame shall not suffer eclipse, nor decay,
But broaden and brighten as years roll away.   (3)

1. "During about ten days they resisted the most strenuous exertions of assailants," &c.—Miles' *History of Canada*, page 117.

2. Parkman, in his *Pioneers of France in the New World*, says, in a foot-note (p. 321): "According to Lafitau, both bucklers and breast-plates were in frequent use among the Iroquois. The former were very large, and made of cedar wood covered with interwoven thongs of hide."

3. In this ballad, the writer has purposely omitted to recognize the part taken in the affair by the few Algonquin and Huron Indians who joined the Frenchmen. First, because nearly the whole number deserted to the enemy during the conflict, thus more than counterbalancing any service which they may have rendered at the outset, and, second, because the contrast of race and character is lost by mixing civilized and savage men together as allies in opposition to combatants of the latter type. For these reasons, he ventures to think that the spirit of poesy will justify this deviation from the strict line of historical narration.

CHANGE ON THE OTTAWA.

(A Fragment.)

I.

Onward the Saxon treads.   Few years ago,
   A chief of the Algonquins passed at dawn,
With knife, and tomahawk, and painted bow,
   Down the wild Ottawa, and climbed upon
A rocky pinnacle, where in the glow
   Of boyhood he had loved to chase the fawn ;
Proudly he stood there, listening to the roar
Of rapids sounding, sounding evermore.

II.

All else was silence, save the muffled sound
   Of partridge drumming on the fallen tree,
Or dry brush crackling from the sudden bound
   Of startled deer, that snorts, and halts to see,

Then onward o'er the leaf-encumbered ground,
　　Through his green world of beauty, ever free.
Such was the scene—no white man's chimney nigh,
And joy sat, plumed, in the young warrior's eye.

III.

No white man's axe his hunting grounds had marred,
　　The primal grandeur of the solemn woods,
When Summer all her golden gates unbarred,
　　And hung voluptuous o'er the shouting floods,—
Or when stern Winter gave the rich reward,
　　All suited with his uncorrupted moods,
For all was built, voiced, roofed with sun and cloud,
By the Great Spirit unto whom he bowed.

IV.

The grey of morn was edging into white,
　　When down the rugged rock the Indian passed,
Like a thin shadow. Soon the rosy light
　　Lay on the maple leaf, the dew-drops cast
A lustrous charm on many a mossy height,
　　And squirrels broke out in chatter, as the blast
Swayed the tall pine tops where they leaped, and made
Grand organ-music in the green-wood shade.

v.

Again the Indian comes—some years have rolled,—
   Down the wild Ottawa, and stands upon
His boyhood haunt, and with an eye still bold
   Looks round, and sighs for glories that are gone ;
For all is changed, except the fall that told,
   And tells its Maker still, and Bird-rock lone ;
Sadly he leans against an evening sky,
Transfigured in its ebb of rosy dye.

VI.

He sees a city there :—the blazing forge,
   The mason's hammer on the shaping stone,
Great wheels along the stream revolving large,
   And swift machinery's whirr and clank, and groan,
And the fair bridge that spans the yawning gorge,
   Which drinks the spray of Chaudière, leaping prone,—
And spires of silvery hue, and belfry's toll,
All strike, like whetted knives, the red man's soul.

VII.

Wide the area of the naked space
   Where broods the city like a mighty bird,
And the grave Sachem from his rock can trace

Her flock of villages, where lately stirred
The bear and wolf, tenacious of their place,
   And where the wild cat with her kittens purred ;—
Now while the shades of eve invest the land,
What myriad lights flash out on every hand !

VIII.

The dead day's crimson, interwove with brown,
   Has wrapped the watcher upon Oiseau Rock,
And o'er him hangs bright Hesper, like a crown,
   As if the hand of Destiny would mock
His soul's eclipse and sorrow-sculptured frown ;—
   Thick as wild pigeons, dusky memories flock
O'er the wide wind-fall of his fated race,
And thus he murmurs to his native place :

IX.

" Here dwelt within the compass of my gaze,
   All whom I ever loved, and none remain
To cheer the languor of my wintry days,
   Or tread with me across the misty plain ;
A solitary tree, the bleak wind strays
   Among my boughs, which moaningly complain ;
Familiar voices whisper round and say,
Seek not to find our graves! Away! Away!

X.

The sire who taught my hands to hold the bow,
   The mother who was proud of my renown,
On them no more the surly tempests blow,
   How little do they heed or smile or frown,
The summer's blossoms or the winter's snow !
   With them, at last, I thought to lay me down,
Where birds should sing, and wild deer safely play,
And endless woods fence out the glare of day.

XI.

Friend of my youth, my " Wa-Wa* Height," adieu !
   No more shall I revisit thee, no more
Gaze from thy summit on the upper blue,
   And listen to the rapid's pleasing roar ;—
I go,—my elder brother !—to pursue
   The Elk's great shadow on a distant shore,
Where Nature, still unwounded, wears her charms,
And calls me, like a mother, to her arms."

XII.

He ceased and strode away ; no tear he shed,
   A weakness which the Indian holds in scorn,
But sorrow's moonless midnight bowed his head,

And once he looked around—Oh ! so forlorn !
I hated for his sake the reckless tread
　Of human progress,—on *his* race no morn,
No noon of happiness shall ever beam ;
They fade as from our waking fades a dream.

*Wa-Wa, *or i.e. lit.—the Wild Goose.*

THE BLIND MINSTREL OF THE MARKET PLACE.

Along the echoing harbour crowds appear,
For 'tis the busy season of the year ;
Soft airs of June are whispering to the leaves,
And happy swallows sport along the eaves.
Far, hovering on the east's remotest rim,
A white-winged ship is seen, sublimely dim ;
Half on the watery plain and half in heaven,
No fairer vision to the world is given.
At nearer view, her topmast gives the breeze
St. George's Cross, renowned o'er all the seas ;
Slowly she paces up the shimmering tide,
Britannia's peerless child, old ocean's bride ;
With majesty of mien she takes her place,
While welcome beams on many a wishful face ;
Sweet thoughts of distant scenes, forever dear,
Her presence brings to many a wanderer here

Scenes which, however fair his lot be cast,
The exile loves and longs for to the last.
The jovial sailor, safe from ocean's roar,
Sings on the deck, or gaily leaps on shore ;
Careless of dangers past or to be met,
His wish upon the present chance is set ;
If Prudence speaks, her voice is hushed to rest,
His only business now is to be blest.
Such was the aspect of the genial hour
When first I felt the sightless minstrel's power,
And gazed upon that melancholy brow
Which moved the pitying tear, and haunts me now.
Stricken, but aye serene, he gropes his way
Where busy hucksters all their wealth display,
And prudent housewives roam from stall to stall,
Till each has higgled round the range of all.
Youthful, yet worn, his pallid cheek betrays
That he has borne the pinch of evil days ;
His inner world, a lonely isle of thought,
Afflicted with an unpropitious lot ;
His outer world, a blank,—contracted, strange,—
The breadth his hand can reach, its utmost range.
The landscape, stretching to the purple hills,
With groves and cottages and gleaming rills,

All nice gradations that belong to space,
And which the humblest rustic loves to trace,
If mentioned or described, perplex his mind,
And force the silent comment, *I am blind !*—
In vain for him the splendour of the skies
Expanded floats above his lifted eyes.
The blush of dawn, the noontide beams, the hues
That clothe the west when fall the early dews,—
These, and the softer glories of the night,
Send no sweet message through his torpid sight.

But never having known the joy that springs
From observation of external things,
To him their absence is but partial loss,
And half unconsciously he bears his cross.
Taught, by a lofty faith, to nurse content,
And prize the scanty good that God hath lent,
He trusts the sacred source of perfect love,
And hopes to see the light in worlds above.
Thus safely anchored, bravely doth he try
To earn the little that his wants supply,
Nursing the manly virtue in his heart,
That scorns the mendicant's ignoble part.
His violin, the only wealth he owns,

Speaks to his soul in such endearing tones,
That now, the sole companion of his life,
He names, in quiet jest, *My little wife.*

To-day, while sounds of commerce everywhere,
And hasty human footsteps jar the air,
Upon the market-place the minstrel stands,
Tuning his instrument with pallid hands.
Close by, the mighty river rolls along,
And, solaced by its sympathetic song,
He hastens, while his audience gather round,
To emulate the sweetness of its sound.
With practised ear, in listening attitude,
He first interrogates the vocal wood ;
Its answers he receives with changing look,
Anger, approval, pleasure, or rebuke.
Till coaxing, fondling, with persuasive art,
Pressing the yearner closer to his heart,
The perfect soul of harmony he wakes,
And o'er his face the light of gladness breaks.
So must he regulate his rude desires,
Who fain would tread the earth as heaven requires ;
Each captive vice must cower beneath his skill.
Till made the pliant vassal of his will,

Then angels, though unseen, will linger near,
And whisper secrets of their native sphere.

Now speeds the bow, and from the panting strings
Sweet meanings float afar on airy wings.
No complicated task doth he assume,
Such as may suit the genius of a Prume,
But simple airs that charm the simple heart,
Partaking more of nature than of art ;
Soft sounds and plaintive murmurs that express
All earnest feelings, rapture, and distress,
Love's fever and the patriotic glow
That prompts the eager hand to smite the foe ;
But chief the nimble notes that youthful feet,
So dear to Terpsichora, love to greet,
Inspire his elbow ;—how it swirls and sways,
As if to trace the dance's witching maze !
The young, the aged, homely face and fair,
With shining looks and willing ears are there ;
The market-woman, dowered with double chin,
And proud rotundity of abdomen ;
The scented dandy, with his twirling cane,
Embroidered vest, and gorgeous golden chain ;
The bare-foot urchin, with his mottled face,

Elbowing Master Ruffle for a place ;—
There, girt with scarlet sash, with whip in hand,
The modest *habitant* secures his stand ;—
A gentle being, blessed with quiet days,
Politeness blossoms out in all his ways :—
O, ye who walk, and sit, and speak by rule !
Forgetting Nature's free and ample school,
In him behold, and copy if you can,
The royal pattern of a *gentleman*.

Vain the attempt to sketch the motley ring,
Enough that generous fingers freely fling
Such tokens as confess the minstrel's skill,
And testify how sweet is music's thrill.
Then long may he survive to wield the bow,
And muse beside the river's rushing flow,
Apollo's heir—his territorial space,
The full circumference of the Market Place.

W. H. MAGEE.

(A friend of early days.)

You saw, my friend, when last we met,
  Time's sober reckoning on my face ;
  But neither time nor change of place
Can cause my spirit to forget
  One honest throb, one living trace
Of friendship, till life's sun shall set,——

Such friendship as I've found in you,·-
  A glory that unites and binds
  The poetry of kindred minds,
Forever stedfast, ever true.

The years are drifting fast and far ;
  We half-way hear the haunted river
  Whose monody is, *Never, never!*
We half-discern the misty bar

Past which no soul returneth ever;
Our lamp is not the morning star.

Nor can we of our lot complain;
  We've had of bliss an ample share;
  We banquet on ambrosial fare
And nectar wines of heart and brain.

No heritage of goods or lands
  We owe to an ancestral line;
  Obedient to the voice divine,
We earn our bread with willing hands.

No drones nor parasites are we;
  And hence brave comrade, you and I
  Can lift our foreheads to the sky
And plead our lawful right, *to be*,—
  To be, enjoy, and sternly try
To leave the world more fair and free

Than when upon its round we fell,—
  Two feeble rays that wandered far
  From nebula, or hidden star—
Whence? wherefore? whither? who can tell?

We only know that we are here,
    That life is brief and death is sure ;
    That it is noble to endure,
And keep the eye of conscience clear.
    Will love and knowledge ever cure
The evils of this troubled sphere ?

We look in Nature's face, and doubt
    Whether she means us good or ill ;
    We know that she can stab and kill,
And blow our taper-joys all out.

An angel and a fiend by turns,
    A grace, a fury,—all we find
    As shapings of the human mind
In her strange aspect shines and burns ;
    One moment infinitely kind ;
The next, a breaking heart she spurns.

Her lightnings smite ; her arctic breath
    Congeals the traveller's blood, and lo,
    He sinks into a tomb of snow !
No prayer can bribe the clutch of death.

She lets her savage cyclones loose,
   She bids her flaming lavas flow,
   And sudden as a ruffian's blow
Great cities perish ! What excuse?
   Does God, indeed, ordain it so ?
Is not the problem more abstruse ?

If we but mark how finely blend
   The foul and fair, the dark and bright
   That in this Mother-Sphinx unite,
We may believe her still our friend.

Excessive beauty floods the sky,
   And earth is fair through all the year;—
   In autumn, when the woods are sere,
In winter, when the white winds fly,
   And blow their trumpets far and near,
There's beauty for a loving eye.

The sculptor, in long ages past,
   Enamoured, taxed his glorious art
   That he might press his hungry heart
To Nature's charms, and hold her fast.

Like him, we shall not fail to find
   On earth, in sky, in air, in sea,
   Many a dazzling deity,
If pure in heart, and great in mind.

Then let us live as best we may,
   And bid our souls ascend, and sing
   Like birds and brooks that greet the spring.
Shall we be found less wise than they?
   Hence, Care, upon thy ebon wing !
I'm happy with my friend to-day.

LINES.

(Written on recovering from the effects of a serious accident.)

I.

I felt the cold shadow
    Of Death as he passed,
And counted that horrible
    Moment my last.

No fear of a Future
    Took part in the play
Of thoughts that were losing
    The sweet light of day.

A shock and a tumult,—
    A crash and a strife,—
And all that pertains to
    The aim of my life

Swept o'er me and through me,
   As if to remind
I had housed with the sluggard,
   And loitered behind.

If this penance hath hinted
   The value of time,
Hath taught me to reckon
   Delay as a crime,

The days yet uncounted
   May balance the cost
Of all I have suffered,
   Of more than I've lost.

II.

When the Demon of Torture
   O'ertakes and assails,
And thy skill, Cotyæus!
   But little avails;

What is it that sheddeth
   The balm of relief?
What anodyne softens
   The pain and the grief?

LINES.

'Tis the presence of friendship,
  The clasp of a hand,
'Tis the kindness that speaketh
  In tones to command

The Demon to loosen
  His hold and depart,
That Hope may return to
  Her nest in the heart.

This boon have I tasted
  While couched in my room;
And fair, as the rainbow
  That spanneth the gloom,

Shall be the remembrance
  Of faces that shed
A magic that blunted
  The thorns of my bed,
That wrought on the Demon
  Of pain till he fled.

HALLOWE'EN IN CANADA;

AND

HOW IT SETTLED A DOMESTIC QUARREL.

To-night, upon the land or sea,
Wherever Scotland's bairns may be,
Whether they plough Australian soil,
Or in Canadian forests toil ;—
Or, on the Ganges or the Nile,
Defy the gaping crocodile ;
Or on the South Sea waters sail,
A terror to the fated whale ;
In lonely dell or crowded street,
Wherever two or more may meet,
Warm hands are clasped—no formal grip,—
No dainty, bloodless fingers' tip,
But such a cordial squeeze and shake
As leave behind a welcome ache,
Such greeting as can only mean,
To-night, my friend, is Hallowe'en.

The quicksand of the sliding years,
Is moistened with perpetual tears ;
But as the sunshine tempers showers,
As perfume clings to wounded flowers,
As music tones the midnight storm,
As beauty clothes the lightning's form,
So wedded to each human ill,
   Some pleasing charm is felt or seen,
And hence, though exiles here, they thrill
   With yearly joys of Hallowe'en.

But in this logic-leavened age,
When every boot-black is a sage,
When naught but the electric wire,
Or steam-propulsion can inspire,—
When lovers travelling to the moon,
Are married in a great balloon,*
"What folly," says my neighbour wise,
A cyclopædia in his eyes,
" What superstition to uphold
This Hallowe'en, so ghostly, old,
A custom suit for infant schools,
Gray dotards, and the mob of fools."

  * An instance of such performance was reported in the public prints at the time when these lines were written.

Just hearken to a truthful story
  Of two plain folk who dwelt alone,
  To city shows and glare unknown,
A forest life their only glory,
  Then judge, ye unbelieving crew,
  What faith in Hallowe'en can do.

THE QUARREL.

Tam Gregg and Jean, a thrifty pair,
He lithe and tall, she plump and fair,
Far westward in the wild woods' shade,
A comfortable home had made,
And lived for years, true man and wife,
Without a single word of strife.
Till one day, with the toothache crossed,
His even temper Tammy lost,
And glowered, and snarled, and snapped, and swore,
And stamped upon the cottage floor,
Kicked the poor dog, and cuffed the wean,
And knit his angry brows at Jean.
At length some bitter words he said
  Which fell like fire-flakes on her heart,
And turned her cheek from pale to red,

When bouncing up with sudden start,
She hurried from his evil view ;
  And with hot purpose inly vowed
That Tam his spiteful fling should rue.
For she was Highland born, and proud,
  And boasted the McGregor blood,
  Now coursing like a fiery flood
Through all her veins : her heart throbs loud,
  But careless if its chambers burst,
Her head upon her hot hands bowed,
She thought: " Weel, Tam, you've said your worst,
And even if it holds a week,
I winna look at you, nor speak,
Till sorry for the wrang ye've done,
  A wrang that would provoke the Deil,
Ye bend your hough, and seek to wun
  Forgiveness for the pangs I feel."
Three days crept past, they slept and woke,
And neither to the other spoke ;—
Three wretched days, with sunless eye
Each passed the other coldly by,
  Like shadows in a pantomime ;
  And in that silent lapse of time,
What thoughts, what griefs, were known to each,

Conjecture only scarce may reach.
The woods, but lately green, were bare,
And moaning winds were wandering there ;
Their feathered guests had ceased to sing,
And southward flew on chilly wing ;
Dark clouds obscured the sickly light,
And night seemed death, and day seemed night.
Sad signals these, and o'er the change
The vacant looks of both would range,
While Love, slow pointing to the past,
Asked each, " Must this forever last? "

Jean still maintained her stately tread,
But Tam grew sad, and drooped his head,
That uncombed, mop-like, sandy pow,
That never looked so wild as now.
He twitched his beard and peeped askance,
In hopes to catch some random glance
Of Jean's blue eyes, but there, O, fate !
The sullen lids seemed charged with hate,
And curdled scorn, and wounded pride.
But anxious still the truth to hide,
His reasoning all perversely ran ;
" If guilty, am I not a man ?

And is it not a woman's place
To yield with a relenting grace?"
Thus did he manage still to frown
And fight his best convictions down.
The fourth day fell on Hallowe'en,
And now remorse and anguish keen,
Like wild cats seized on Tammy's mind.
A moment's peace he could not find.
All day he shuffled in and out,
And snuffed, and coughed, and glowered about,
And tried to whistle, but his lips,
As dry as two sun-seasoned chips,
Refused to pucker :—what a look,
When baffled thus, his visage took !
The gloaming hour drew on, and Tam
Was seated by the chimney jamb.
His eyes were bent upon the fire,
And, listening to his heart's desire,
" To-night," thought he, " is Hallowe'en,
    Seven years ago this very night
I first beheld my comely Jean,
    And courted her till morning's light.
O happy, happy hours ! and now !"—
He struck his hand against his brow,

When suddenly a gladsome thought
He from the glowing cinders caught.—
Two nuts with eager hand he drew
   From forth his pouch, and muttering low,
" *That's her, that's me,*" he gently threw
   The orbs of fate amid the glow
Of golden fire upon the hearth,
   And watched them with such eager gaze,
As if his all of heaven and earth
   Depended on their puny blaze.
" Now," whispered Tam, " if I but lean
My kindled kindness toward my Jean,
If over her my flamelet spread,
No matter how she bear her head,
Then must I be the first to speak,
And press repentance on her cheek."
The nuts caught fire, and Tam's at first
Swelled up as if its sides would burst ;
But instantly a blaze shot out,
And reached and clasped his Jean about,
And round her never ceased to play,
Till both in ashy cinders lay.
" Enough," cried Tam, with moistened eye,
" Thus may we live, and love, and die,
And thus at last together lie ! "

Meantime, poor Jean, sore sick at heart,—
Though mindful of her vow and smart,
Began to feel her purpose fail,
And, strolling out among the kail,
She conjured up some soft excuse
For tooth-afflicted Tam's abuse.
So came it, as the fates decreed,
She with herself and Heaven agreed
To take her chance, by pulling out
A kail stalk, which, " if tall and stout,
Then must Tam Gregg come ben and speak,
But otherwise if slim and weak,
I'll take it as a solemn proof
That I maun first hold out my loof."
Her eyes she bandaged, groped about,
Perturbed with many a tender doubt,
And mindless of the gain or cost,
Cared little if she won or lost.
Just then, as Tam the garden gained,
He spied her, and his heart was pained,
For scarcely could he understand
 Whether his wife was daft or wise,
Groping around with shaky hand,
Her apron tied across her eyes.

With open mouth amazed he stood,
  And watched her, all remorseful now,
  The big veins throbbing on his brow,
Till she her verdict clutched, then rude,
Tore off the bandage from her sight,
And frowning, smiling, red, and white,
Confessed her prize a puny thing,
  But little thicker than her thumb;
So must she cower her haughty wing,
  And hold her lips no longer dumb.
Still wondering what the lass could mean,
  Tam stole upon her ere she knew,
Exclaiming fondly, " Jean ! why, Jean !"
  His arm around her waist he threw.
No sooner done, no sooner said,
Than on his breast she leaned her head,
And wept like any child ;—But no,
Our story must not further go,
Except to add, that tall Tam Gregg,
Grown wild with gladness, shook his leg,
And joked, and laughed and filled his cup,
And threw his auld blue bonnet up,
And kissed the bairn, and Jean, and sang,
Till through the woods such echoes rang,

That prowling catamount and bear,
Fled frightened to their distant lair.
Each learned the other's plot and plan,
And through their veins such rapture ran,
That heedless of their recent pain,
They almost wished to quarrel again.

So ends the tale, and if I've shown,
That though the world has wiser grown,
A loving heart and generous mind
Some good in Hallowe'en may find,—
Then, Caledonians, prize it still,
 And whether on the land or sea,
 Your scattered homes may chance to be,
Maintain it with a right good will.

Old Scotia ! Though they never more
May stand upon thy rugged shore,—
The lofty fame which thou hast won,
The daring deeds thy sons have done,
Thy storied glens, and streams, and heights,
Where heroes fought for freeman's rights,
And stubborn as the will of fate,
Maintained their independent state,—

These, feeding still their patriot fire,
Will never let the flame expire ;
And when, beneath a foreign sky,
Some home-nursed trifle meets the eye,—
A simple bluebell from the glen
Where trod the feet of "Cameron men,"
Or white-cheeked daisy from the braes
Where Burns exhaled his thrilling lays ;—
A sigh will rise, a tear will start,
And every prompting of the heart,
Though half the globe should intervene,
Will teach them evermore, I ween,
To meet and hold their Hallowe'en.

ETHEL.

Little sky-waif, come astray
Twice twelve months ago to-day!
What a world of joy is thine !
What a glow of summer shine
Cheers the house wherein thou art,
Sly magician of the heart !

In those large, those azure eyes,
All the splendour of the skies,
All the beauty that belongs
To the poet's sweetest songs,
All the wisdom known and lost
That the wisest sage could boast,
Beam and lure and half reveal
Secrets that the gods conceal.

See those ringlets all unshorn
That her pretty neck adorn ;—
Golden hues and silken gloss
On the charmèd air they toss
Sun-gleams in a starry spray.—
Dearest little laughing fay !

See her tiny feet beat time,
In an ecstasy of rhyme,
To the pearly notes that win
From the speaking violin.
See her fingers, dimpled, white,
Mimic with a grave delight
Those that wonderingly she sees
Race along the ivory keys.

Hear her prattle, indistinct ;—
Much we guess at, still we think
It may be some long lost speech
That she fondly strives to teach,—
Language known to airy things,
It may chance, whose spirit wings
In a merry mischief keep
Little human elves from sleep.

13

ETHEL.

Ask her father, ask her mother,
They will vouch there is no other,
Never was on land or sea
Such a charming girl as she.
Surely they who know her best
Must the simple truth attest;
But if further proof you seek,
Let her solemn grandpa speak.—
He a mighty oath will swear,
By the silver in his hair!
By his sober-sided muse!
All good people needs must choose
Make confession, that for grace,
Loveliness of form and face,
Ways so simple, yet so wise,
Large-eyed Ethel takes the prize.

KEATS.

Full late in life I found thee, glorious Keats !
   Some chance blown verse had visited my ear
   And careless eye, once in some sliding year,
Like some fair-plumaged bird one rarely meets.

And when it came that o'er thy page I bent,
   A sudden gladness smote upon my blood ;—
   Wonder and joy, an aromatic flood,
Distilled from an enchanted firmament.

And on this flood I floated, hours and hours,
   Unconscious of the world's perplexing din,
   Its blackened crust of misery and sin,
Rocked in a shallop of elysian flowers.

All melodies of earth and heaven are thine.
   That one so young such music could rehearse
   As swells the undulations of thy verse
Is what Hyperion only might define.

The voices of old pines, the lulling song
   Of silver-crested waterfalls, the sweep
   Of symphonies that swell the booming deep
To thy immortal minstrelsy belong.

Nor less the whispered harmony that falls,
   Like twilight dews, from heaven's starry arch,
   For gentle souls that listen to the march
Of airy footfalls in ethereal halls.

Unhappy, happy Keats ! A bitter sweet
   Was thy life's dream ; death grinning at thy heels,
   While Fame, before thee, smiled her grand appeals,
Tempting to dizzy heights thy winged feet.

Methinks thou didst resemble (over-bold
   May be the fancy) thy Endymion,—
   Now charmed with earth-born beauty and anon
Finding some imperfection in the mould.

He sued a heaven-born splendor to allay
   The hunger and the fever of his heart ;
   And thus to Cynthia he did impart
The fearful secret of his misery.

Oh, had I missed this Hippocrene, and slept
   Without full measure of the choicest draught
   That ever mortal man divinely quaffed,
What depth of bliss the Gods from me had kept !

THE CRISIS.*

The roar of battle peals afar.
In lurid haze, the Northern star
Gleams through the flaming clouds of war ;
   Death rides the burning blast.

What havoc on the groaning plain !
What never ending heaps of slain !
What tepid pools of purple rain !—
   We look, and stand aghast.

And still the strife resounds abroad,
Earth trembles, and her forests nod,
As if she felt the stamp of God,
   And heard His voice at last.

* These lines were written in reference to the American civil war, at the time known as "Grant's Battles in the Wilderness," when, in a note to the War Department ,(May 11, 1864), he penned those memorable words, " I propose to fight it out on this line, if it takes all summer.

He speaks, indeed! Who hath an ear
To learn His will, may hark and hear
These hallowed words, to freedom dear,
   Tyrants, release the slave!

And till that mandate is obeyed,
May Northern hearts beat undismayed,
And all the world, with generous aid,
   Cheer on the loyal brave.

Ha! o'er the Southern plains shall spread
The children of the honoured dead,
And evermore above their head
   The dear old flag shall wave;—

Shall wave with all its stars, a sign
That though the hosts of hell combine,
The cause of freedom is divine,
   And slavery must expire.

A sign that, not in vain, the great
And good of every clime and state
Have battled with a bloody fate.
   Breathing heroic fire.

THE CRISIS.

I love the flag, because it flings
Defiance in the face of kings,
While Liberty expands her wings
   To crown the world's desire.

IN MEMORY OF JOSEPH GUIBORD.

1875.

The storm of six long years is past,
And peacefully he rests at last.—
Thrice hearsed, thrice cursed, let honest fame
Blow treble honour to his name.
If endless years of praise ensue,
'Tis but the hero's earthly due.
The humble printer's mighty art,
   Though banned, will vindicate her son,
And tell to every truthful heart
   While woods grow green and waters run—
That he who braves a despot's frown
Will wear at length the victor's crown ;
Even when slain, and torn asunder,
And scattered piecemeal, trodden under

The brutal feet of frenzied foes,
His deeds will rise, as Christ's arose,
And, borne upon the chainless air,
Will plead for freedom everywhere.

Let curses from their rookery fly,
    And flap their foul wings o'er his bones,
    The autumn wind that round him moans
Will mock them, while in vain they try
    To penetrate those friendly stones.

Come what might come, from man or elf,
He dared not quarrel with himself,
Nor stab the Truth that in his breast
Had found a warm and welcome nest.
No terrors of the burning lake,
    Fancied or real, beyond the grave,
Nor purgatorial flames could shake
    His manly soul, so firm and brave,
    For he was neither fool nor slave.
True to himself, he lived and died,
Not wilful, nor elate with pride,
But steadfast in his honest thought,
Self-justified, self-ruled, self-taught.

Our Brother ! wheresoever now
Thy spirit lifts its free-born brow,
Behold thy kindred !—not alone
In Canada will thousands own
    Relationship ; throughout all lands,—
    Wherever freedom shines or dawns,
    An army with uplifted hands,
Constrained by glowing links that bind
Nobility of mind to mind,
    Will crown thee with their benisons.

Thus Guibord ! shall the commonwealth
    Of truth's and reason's fearless sons,—
Scorners of men who think by stealth,
    Now hold thee in fraternal trust,
    And consecrate thine injured dust,
While woods grow green and water runs.

IT MOVES.

" I know it moves," so said the man
   Whose genius read the astral scroll
   From east to west, from pole to pole,
Yet, under a terrific ban,

Denied his thought, the truth denied,
   And crushed in soul betwixt the strife
   Of love of truth and love of life,
To silence doomed he slowly died.

Since that dark hour, 'tis joy to know,
   The thoughts of fearless men have moved
   As move the stars ; the years have proved
Thy deathless worth, Galileo !

What marvel if he shrank with dread
   Beneath the lifted iron hand
   Whose marks were seen on every land,—
Red marks where truest seers had bled.

The glare of Bruno's fiery shroud
   Still seemed to haunt the midnight skies,
   And falling on his menaced eyes,
His head the noble Pisan bowed.

And who the number may compute
   Of kindred souls, whose secret fears
   Have held them captive all their years,
And kept their lips forever mute?

Grim Persecution's sleepless rage
   Has many guises, all the same
   In essence, differing but in name,
O'er all the earth, from age to age.

And if less potent now for harm,
   Let Freedom's watchmen guard her towers ;
   Happy to cry the all-well hours,
Ready to ring the prompt alarm.

Low sinks the race where thought and speech
   Are helpless slaves to crown and cross ;
   Where heresy brings blame and loss ;
And each is set a spy on each.

Blest is the soil where men can stand
 And say it is a crime to hide
 The light of reason, to deride
The one sure Deity's command—

The voice of Conscience ;—here to-night
 This heritage of centuries, old
 And new, in sacred trust we hold :
Our watchword—" Freedom and the Right."

SUPERSTITION.

O Superstition, could the world behold
   Thy wrinkled visage,—worshipped as thou art,
Not all the pomp of earth, nor all its gold
   Could purchase for thee one devoted heart;
The sons of science, eloquently bold,
   Have felt the strokes of thy unsparing dart,
And knaves despotic, kneeling at thy shrines,
Have made thy slaves the tools of their designs.

To science turn; she cultivates the rough
   And barren regions of the savage mind,
Her lore is not the visionary stuff
   Of gloomy monks; blind leaders of the blind.
Her ways are mild and beautiful enough
   To melt the rigour of a heart unkind,
Her truths are diamonds, such as will endure
Throughout all ages, palpable and sure.

VIGER SQUARE.*

Here in this quiet garden shade,
　　Whose blossoms spread their bloom before me,
The world's gay cheats,—Life's masquerade,
Like evil ghosts from memory fade,
And calm and holy thoughts come o'er me.

Ambrosial haunt; the orient light
　　Falls golden on thy soft seclusion ;
And like the lone and shadowy night,
Grim care, abashed, has taken flight,
　　And joys gleam forth in rich profusion.

These odorous flowers that feast the bee,
　　Those mimic fountains sunward leaping,
And yon red-berried rowan tree,
That brings my childhood back to me,
　　With hallowed scenes of Memory's keeping.

* A beautiful public park, in the east end of Montreal.

All these, and more, with beauty clad,
  Invite the city's weary mortals—
The pale-faced maid, the widow sad,
The sinking merchant, growing mad,
  To muse within these peaceful portals.

Here is the stone that sages sought,
  Here the famed lamp of blest Aladdin;
Objects that tell ambitious thought,
" All that thy greed hath ever caught
  Cannot like us, console and gladden."

14

1881.

Year of all years, that hath been unto me
 More bitter than the depths of Acheron,
 I will not curse thee for the ill thou'st done,
But bow as best I may to thy decree.

With what a buoyancy of hope and trust
 I gave thee generous welcome at thy birth,
 Swelling the chorus of the general mirth ;
And thou my greeting hast returned with—dust !

Two happy eyes that shone upon thy dawn,
 And beamed upon us from our chamber door
 Are quenched, and closed to open nevermore—
The face, the form, the loving voice is gone.

Go, savage and inexorable year !
 Haste to the gloomy Hades of the Past !
 Not to thy memory are these moanings cast,
Not for thy exit falls the hasty tear.

DESPONDENT.

(Occasioned by hearing a pathetic air played on the Flute.)

Oh! cease, sweet Minstrel, cease to play,
   My eyes with tears are filling fast;
I see life's pleasures fade away,
   I feel misfortune's coldest blast.

Thy witching strain is sad and sweet,
   I cannot bear its melting sound;
It tells of joys that passed too fleet,
   And early loves in sorrow drowned.

I see the ranks of early years
   Like awful spectres pass along;
I see a dismal lake of tears,
   I hear lost Hope's expiring song.

DESPONDENT.

Then cease, Musician ! cease to play,
My heavy heart is filled with grief;
And every note but seems to say—
The world for me has no relief.

THOMAS D'ARCY McGEE.

April 7th, 1868.)

There is mourning to-day in the halls of the great,
And homes of the people of lowly estate.
A deed has been done which o'ershadows the heart
With a darkness and horror that will not depart.—
The Poet and Statesman lies cold in his gore,
His eloquent accents will thrill us no more :
No more, with our hearts to all charities strung,
Shall we listen to catch the sweet sounds of his tongue.
That tongue,whose enchantment could hold us in thrall
Will never more gladden the close, crowded hall ;
But the light of his genius will shine o'er the land,
And his fame, like Mount Royal, forever shall stand,
For his thoughts were the lights of our northern sky,
And the soul's spoken melody never can die.
O God ! could no virtue, no pity restrain

The wretch who has sown such a harvest of pain?
What though on the scaffold he die for the deed
That causes fond hearts, like his victim, to bleed?
A million such lives no atonement can make
For the star that is quenched, for the sorrows that
    shake
Our trust in the highest and holiest plan,
Our faith in the ultimate goodness of man.

THE NEWS-BOY.

Hark on the street the News-boy's call,
  Above all other sounds it rings ;
" Great news by telegraph " * he brings,
  A luxury devoured by all ;
And some with vacant visage laugh ;—
  Laugh while they read of ruthless war,
  Of huge disasters, near and far,
  Of crimes that give the world a jar,
O wondrous news by telegraph !

The Press is modern Jove, and he
  Swift Mercury, who bears abroad
  The utterance of the sleepless god,
Wherever thriving cities be ;
Wherever steeples pierce the sky ;

*This was written in the early days of telegraphing, when the News-
boy delighted to proclaim that his papers, sparkled with intelligence,
flashed along the electric wire.

Where desperate politicians bawl,
Responsive to their country's call,
And drunkards reel against the wall,
There peals the eager News-boy's cry.

Through central and suburban part
He hurries on, and who may tell
What hopes his little bosom swell,
What distant visions warm his heart.
At times you see him—hapless one!
With elbows out, a tuft of hair
Seeking, through crown-rent hat, the air,
His feet half shod, or wholly bare,
And buttons of importance gone.

But whether ragged, spruce or grand,
Proudly his pile of pence he jinks,
And, reckoning his profits, thinks :—
"The day may come when I shall stand
Among the richest and the best."
And then his troubles, light as chaff,
Pass from him; he could leap and laugh ;
"Great news, great news, by telegraph !"
Again he shouts with swelling chest.

And thus his rill of boyhood runs ;
  And oft dependent on his mite,
  A widowed mother waits at night,
Waits with her famished little ones,
And listens for his homeward tread.
  A happy smile illumes her face ;
  The mother and the boy embrace,
  And, all within the humble place,
A sudden light from Heaven is shed.

He tells her of the day's success,
  Of incidents both grave and gay,
  The dandy's hat that flew away,
And wind-tossed ladies in distress.
The widow gazes while he speaks ;
  Another voice in his she hears,
  Another face in his appears,
  And holy are the silent tears
That trickle down her pallid cheeks.

But other parents, different far,
  Await the News-boy, and purloin
  The little fellow's honest coin
To spend at some pernicious bar ;

They think not how, with weary tread,
 All day the child has nobly striven'
 To merit praise ;—with curses driven,
 A scanty supper, harshly given,
He weeps within his little bed.

The angels heed his lowly state,
 And pity him, and kindly weave
 A destiny which none perceive,
Save those at the celestial gate.
Then give, my brothers, words of cheer
 To waft the News-boy on his way ;
 His country, at some future day,
 May learn his name, and proudly say :—
Of noblest men he is the peer.

CHARLES HEAVYSEGE.

A man of worth, a man of mind,
Has bade farewell to human kind.
No pomp, no sound of muffled drum,
No multitudes' uncertain hum
Has stirred the air; but stifled sighs,
And gleaming tears and shaded eyes
Are tokens of a reverence felt
For one who to the Muses knelt,
In fealty with noblest vow,
And rose with garland on his brow.

So child-like, modest, reticent,
With head in meditation bent,
He walked our streets !—and no one knew
That something of celestial hue
Had passed along; a toil-worn man
Was seen, no more ; the fire that ran

Electric through his veins and wrought
Sublimity of soul and thought,
And kindled into song, no eye
Beheld until a foreign sky*
Reflected back the wondrous light,
And heralded the poet's might.

Though doomed to less of sun than shade,
No weak complaint he ever made ;
But bravely lived, content to let
The great world roar, and fume, and fret.
In visions of the days of eld
He revelled, and in joy beheld
The glory of the Hebrew sages,
Whose utterance has toned the ages.
The sacred mount, the cave, the stream
Where holy seers were wont to dream,
He knew and loved, and summoned thence
The agents of Omnipotence ;
Fantastic sprites, and buried men
To fight gray battles o'er again.

* The lofty genius of this author attracted no attention in Canada
till noticed by the *North British Review* in an article on his " Saul,"
which appeared in the August number of 1858.

Behold dread Samuel's shade appear!
Behold Goliath's mighty spear !
And lithe-limbed David's sling and stone,
And Saul's fierce madness ; one by one
They rise before us, march, or stand,
Obedient to the Poet's wand.

Dear friend, adieu ! if Malzah-like
An adverse Fate ordained to strike,
Beset thee on life's weary way,
And followed close from day to day,
He failed to conquer, failed to wrest
One murmur from thy manly breast.
Companion of my happiest hours,
Would that my words were fadeless flowers !
That I might lay them on thy tomb
To mitigate its lasting gloom,
And evermore above thee bloom.

BOOKS.

In books I find companionship, they are
My household gods, and naught shall wholly bar
Their voices from me ; from their precious pages
I quaff the immortality of ages.
They are the spirits of the dead, not dumb,
From ancient tombs and monuments they come
To hold communion with the living ; they,
While nations perish and the world grows gray,
Their regal power and pristine beauty keep,
Despite the havoc, and inglorious sleep
Of centuries that bore a crimson hue,—
Despite the flames which they have travelled through,
Unscathed they hold their sceptres, meek they bear
These royal dignities ;—like light and air
They enter, silver-shod, the humblest door,
And breathe their benedictions on the poor.
Ye avatars, true saviours of the world,
Round whom the hopes of wisest souls are curled,

Be mine through life, in pain, or pleasure, mine !
If near me still your pleasant faces shine
The skies may lower—upon my thorny path
The heavens may pour their cataracts of wrath,
I need not falter, need not hold my breath,
Nor tremble at the menaces of Death.

THE DRUNKARD.

He drank ;—
All warning he repelled with scorn.
He boasted his superior strength,
But in the light of manhood's morn
That boasted strength was from him shorn,
His days had measured out their length.

He reeled ;—
And day by day the cheerful sun
Looked kindly on his crooked path,
The nights beheld no credit won,
But brooded over evils done,
And fearful threats and burning wrath.

He fell ;—
A maniac's look he cast around,
Then shook the air with one wild yell,

And smote with bloody hand the ground,
And uttered startling words whose sound
  Ended with blasphemy and hell.

He died ;—
With madness in his blood and brain,
  With curses on his purple lips,
And bloodshot eyes whose every vein
Lay like a red and burning chain,
  As raised by demons' knotted whips.

He lay ;—
Not as the spoils of death are laid,
  When Nature hath no outrage borne,—
Not as the old or young, arrayed
In decent shroud, when calm they fade,
  And honoured by the eyes that mourn.

He lay
Unblest, unprized, uncombed, unwashed,
  A fresh, red, cut was on his brow,
His teeth were set as last they gnashed,
  His eyes glared fierce as last they flashed,
  And few could bear to see him now.

15

His grave !—
I stood beside the Drunkard's grave,
And moralized above the sod
Which rested on the wine-cup's slave,
The dupe of self, whom none could save,
Now left to silence, and his God.

A NIGHT ON THE SKATING RINK.

Our rink is in motion,
Like waves of the ocean,
When Summer shines broad on the sea.
The skaters strike out,
Scarce forbearing to shout,
All happy and joyous and free ;
And the speed of their flight,
Like an arrow of light,
Takes the breath from a laggard like me.

II.

The exquisite whirl
Of that lovely girl
Has tripped up some heart—I fear—
Ah ! were I as young
As when first I sung,

And the rustics were fain to hear,
I would pour out my soul
In a strain that should roll
Aloft to the heavenly sphere.

III.

But though old enough now
To have sons teach me how
To voyage the crystalline floor,
I yield to the power
Of the jubilant hour
And think of my moustache no more ;
For a poet, at least,
Should partake of mirth's feast
Till his top is exceedingly hoar.

IV.

See !—see where she flies,
How adroitly she plies
Those feet with the shining wings,
With a graceful swerve
And a classical curve,
While beneath her the ice-path rings ;

And the wind in a freak
Stops to kiss her fair cheek,
Then around her in ecstacy sings.

v.

Still sweep we around
With a rippling sound,
Keeping time to the orchestra's swell,
Which, like a bright river
Falling headlong forever
O'er a precipice down to the dell,
Bears our troubles far hence,
And entrancing each sense,
Makes the world one melodious spell.

VI.

Let bacchanals drink,
Till like dotards they wink,
Or laugh with a maniac's stare ;
They embrace but the ghost
Of true pleasure, at most,
And their morrow is dark with despair ;
But the health-giving cheer,

That we revel in here,
Makes our lives more enduringly fair.

VII.

So I'm jovial to-night
With the wine of delight,
I am back to my boyhood again ;
For a moment like this
Brings a torrent of bliss
That floods over heart and brain ;
And the era foretold
By the sages of old
Has commenced its millennial reign.

JACK FROST'S HAPPY DREAM.

1883.

In his white world of snow by the northern pole—
   I can point the identical spot on the map—
Jack Frost became weary of working, poor soul,
   So pulled up his collar and pulled down his cap,
   And stretched himself down in his hut for a nap.

Soon snoring he lay, and he dreamt a fine dream
   Of his antics abroad; of whole streets of glare ice,
Where stout ladies falling unthinkingly scream,
   And gray-bearded gallants, exceedingly nice,
   Making haste to assist them, are down in a trice.

Of snow drifts and sleigh-loads of people upset,—
   Roaring sport for the young, but a grief to the old;—
And flying toboggans—the jolliest yet—
   Landing lovers in snow-banks, which out of the cold
   The laughing defiants a moment enfold.

At length in his vision he noticed afar
  Our Crystaline Palace in grandeur arise,
Till it gleamed in mid air like a magical star,
  Creation's last jewel, a thing of the skies,
  And he sprang to his feet in a whirl of surprise.

He swallowed some ice cakes and mounted his steed,
  A Storm, that stood ready to serve at his call,
Strong-winded, and shod with such marvellous speed,
  That he came like the rush of a huge cannon ball,
  Till he brushed the wide border of gay Montreal.

At the Windsor alighting, Jack spied with amaze,
  The Palace translucent that rose in his dream,
Its opaline walls and tall towers ablaze
  With a light that outrivalled Aurora's first beam,
  And he laughed a huge laugh that was more like a
    scream.

And he danced and cut capers around the wide square,
  Like a harlequin, crowing at times like a cock,
His hands on the snow and his feet in the air,
  Till fatigued with his fun, on a glistening block
  Of his own manufacture he sank with a shock.

Then he chuckled and sneezed, and profanely made
    boast—
  In spite of the churches that seemed to protest—
That he hoped in an orthodox fashion to roast,
    If our Palace of Ice was not truly the best
    That ever invited his limbs to take rest.

" And here," said the fellow, " I mean to remain,
    Till this Carnival's over, and then I suppose
I shall have to be off to the Arctic again,
    Where the Wind-god his trumpet in merriment blows,
    And scatters my hail and my harvest of snows."

MONTREAL CARNIVAL SPORTS.

1884.

The Frost-King sat on a throne of snow,
   On a plain in the Royal Isle:
In his hand a sceptre of ice he bore,
On his brow a crown of ice he wore,
   And his face was set in a holiday smile,
When he bade the carnival trumpet blow
For the famous Sports to begin.
The voluble hills returned the din
In echoes that travelled o'er many a mile;
O'er the broad St. Lawrence to St. Helen's Isle,
To the sounding rapids of old Lachine,
To the Boucherville woods with their tufts of green,
And the peaceful hamlets that smiled between.

A multitude vast as the waves of the sea,
When Tritons rejoice that the winds are free,

People from far off Southern lands,
Where the eagle exults on outspread vans,—
   People who came from the prairied West,
And pine-clad East, and numbers untold
Of natives who laughed at the teeth of the cold
   Were there for a gala-day, threefold blest.

The trumpeter wight was an Arctic sprite,
Whose limbs were lank and whose locks were white,
And when he had blown with all his might,
The Frost-King raised his sceptre high,
When it flashed all the lights of a boreal sky,
And thus, in accents of festive tone,
He welcomed the guests who encircled his throne :—

" Friends ! who have journeyed far to share
The verve of our Canadian air,
   Greeting and love to all.
'Tis wise to lay aside each heavy care
   And all the petty ills that do enthral,
To find in ampler scope this lusty joy,
This social amity, where no alloy
Of turbid passion mingles with the gold
   Of kindly fellowship :

Where harmony betwixt the heart and lip
Its primal sanctity delights to hold.
Pleasure is native to the heart of man,
  Here let it freely flow ;
Here let an ocean tide of gladness roll,
Here where no tyrant's interdict can ban
  The sacred glow
That freedom kindles in the human soul.

Now let the *Sports* begin, and first
Let youths and maids who stand athirst
For Canada's supreme sensation,
For motion's wild intoxication,
Launch from yon hills their swift *Toboggans.*
  Behold, upon the utmost crest,
How democratic Jones and Scroggins
  With Lords and Ladies freely jest.
    Blow, trumpet, blow !
    The signal sound how well they know !
Down, down they plunge, what frantic speed !
No lightning-shod celestial steed
E'er swifter clove the azure air
Than headlong down the polished slide
Those young athletes and damsels ride,

Obedient to the trumpet's blare ;
Like foamy waves that seek the shore,
When red-mouthed storms behind them roar,—
Like avalanches loosed from high,—
Like meteors rushing down the sky,—
They spurn the steep, they leap, they fly,
   Till on the flats in bubbling joy they pour.

A *Sport* of more elastic grace
Now claims from us its honoured place.
   Again, my merry sprite,
   The trumpet sound, and let the night
In starry azure veil the face
   Of Earth, enrobed in purest white.
The signal blast the *Skaters* know,
And eagerly—with cheeks aglow,
Their costumes varied as the flowers
And blossoms that the Summer hours
On all the sunny lands bestow—
They skim in joy the crystal floor,
So full their bliss they ask no more.
In sooth it is a goodly show,
Twice twenty hundred twinkling feet
In fairy flight, advance, retreat,

Whilst others, more ambitious still,
In loops and scrolls assert their skill.
The Champion of a hundred rinks,
  Behold him there! his bosom mailed
With trophies rich; what fancy jinks
    Those lithe, light limbs that never failed!
What complicated, airy links
They weave, as weaves a spider's feet!
Till tip-toe wonder, stares and winks,
And plauding hands his triumphs greet.
What ho! what means yon wild array,
In blanket-coats and sashes gay,
With red fire armed, that wind this way?
Stretching afar for many a mile,
Hither they haste in Indian file,
Ha! Ha! the rebel horde I know;
Blow, Trumpeter, the trumpet blow!—
To arms!—the *Snowshoe* host have sworn
To storm our castle walls,—this morn
A faithful courier warning gave;
Defiant let our war-flag wave!
And you, my guests, remain in sight,
Spectators of the weirdest fight
That ever shook the vault of night.

To arms our veterans ! man the walls,
Receive them with a million balls
Of roaring flame, with dart and brand,
And serpents that no mortal hand
Can parry ; let our trusty *Pinch*,
Who never has been known to flinch,
Protect the gates ; our princely friend,
Great *Zero*, shall in wrath defend
The turrets and the loop-holed walls ;
Let *Blizzard*—a tremendous power—
In fury guard the centre tower ;
And *Coldsnap*, thine the task to shower
With fiery hail and blistering squalls,
And cannonade of burning snow
From every point the reeling foe !

The rebels advance with a shout and a cheer ;
  But they reck not the might of that spectral host,
  Each warrior chieftain a blood-freezing ghost,
Who answered their mirth with a jeer.
Strange voices—such sounds as the winter winds make
When lattice and casement they wrench at and shake,
  Were heard in those halls ;
  And such terrible calls

As made the most valiant assailant to quake.
The castle, a lucent volcano, emits
An ocean of flame on the heads of the foe,
They waver—they stagger—they lose their five wits,
And print their appalling defeat in the snow.
Short, sharp and decisive the battle—no breach—
In that marvellous structure the rebels could reach.
To the mountain, abashed, bearing torches, they fled,
Oppressed with the weight of their wounded and dead.
The Frost-King, no longer enveloped in wrath,
With pity surveyed their laborious path ;
And then, to the multitude bending, he said :—

" What folly, what ingratitude !
    To think with such rebellious war
    This wonder of the world to mar !
This temple that in mist and flood
And cataract in embryo slept,
Till near this Royal Island crept
The fluent particles, on which
    I breathed and wedded each to each,
And made the solid lustre rich
    In dazzling beauty, fit to reach
And rival, in these gleaming spires,

The loveliness of astral fires,
The mellow radiance of the moon.
        Ah ! whether late or soon
We with our retinue depart,
Is there a single human heart
Will mourn our exit? Shall we not
Some few months hence be quite forgot?
If even so, another year,
With equal pleasure, equal cheer,
King Frost shall hold his court, we wot,
And meet your warmest welcome here."

PETER WIMPLE'S COURTSHIP.

This poem was written when the author was a pupil of a literary institute in the State of New York, and was read at a public entertainment given by that institution, too long ago to make mention of the date desirable.

I.

Twice forty years have rolled away
Since first I saw the light of day,
And sage experience bids me say,
    Without a grumble,
The youth who yields to woman's sway,
    Down hill will tumble.

II.

While in my "teens," like some of you,
And life's gay colours all were new,
My heart was in a constant stew
    About the fair ;
Though oft a learned friend and true
    Said: "Pete, beware !"

III.

Love songs I scribbled when a lad,
For many a transient choice I had,
Now marching gay, now moping sad,
    Time's flight unheeded ;
A switch, which cures—or kills—the mad,
    Was what I needed.

IV.

My sixteenth summer drawing nigh,
I winked with an experienced eye ;
At church I chanced a maid to spy,
    With beauty blest,
Who made me heave a double sigh,
    And spoiled my rest.

V.

The fairest form of hundreds there,
I gazed upon her graces rare,
And breathed, for once, a pithy prayer,
    In earnest diction.
Some took my wild, unearthly stare
    For deep conviction.

VI.

Oh, how I spent the days ensuing,
With sighs, and groans, and nothing doing
Save weaving plots for instant wooing,
    And sudden marriage!
Meantime the Fates for me were brewing
    A sad miscarriage.

VII.

'Twas summer, and at dawn of day,
When bird to bird gave greeting lay,
Alone I sought the meadows gay,
    Or forest shade,
And there in fancy would portray
    The blue-eyed maid.

VIII.

Each fragrant flower that met my view,
Each pendant drop of glittering dew,
Each little bird that warbling flew
    From spray to spray,
Each bore methought, some semblance true
    Of Jane Levay.

IX.

Her name I carved on fifty trees,
I breathed it to the passing breeze,
And bade the winds o'er all the seas
   To bear it far ;
I fancied her by fond degrees,
   The morning star.

X.

My inward man I felt consume,
My cheeks waxed thin and lost their bloom ;
Some prophesied an early tomb
   Would hide poor Peter ;
I heeded not their words of gloom,
   My thoughts ran sweeter.

XI.

At length it came at gloaming hour,
Dan Cupid strove with all his power,
And sent, at once, a fiery shower
   Through all my frame ;
My shivering nerves could scarce endure
   The scorching flame.

XII.

While thus my youthful marrow fried,
" Ye Gods," said I, " who lovers guide,
This night my charmer must be tried,
         I'll go and see her;
I'll make her my affianced bride,
         My ever-dear."

XIII.

In Sunday trim I soon was dressed,
My clothes, be sure, were not the best,
But people were of humbler taste
         In those good days;
Girls were not pinched about the waist
         By belts or stays,

XIV.

Folk then might go to church or play
In home-made suits of plain sheep-gray,
And no proud fop be heard to say
         " What awkward shapes !"
Those simple times, long fled away,
         Reared no such apes.

XV.

Our sweethearts spun the frocks they wore,
Before their wheels upon the floor
They stepped as lightly evermore
            As belles of France
Who wander from their native shore
            To skip and dance.

XVI.

'Thus Eastern maids, whose vernal bloom
In Homer's verse can ne'er consume,
Assumed the distaff and the loom,
            With cheerful hands;
Their fame is like a sweet perfume
            Of their own lands.

XVII.

But to our theme—too long delayed:
In Sabbath costume now arrayed,
My hat, a gift, of oat-straw braid,
            My kerchief white,
I started as began to fade
            The western light.

XVIII.

I found it hard my thoughts to rally,
　Love's heaven appeared a little squally,
But on the road I made no dally,—
　　My heart was jumping :
You would have vowed it beat to jelly,
　　To have heard it thumping.

XIX.

The whip-poor-will was on the wing,
And " whip-poor-Pete " he seemed to sing,
Yet what such plaguy thought could bring
　　To Peter Wimple?
I gave my head a manly swing,
　　At whim so simple.

XX.

The waters of my own loved stream—
The Hudson—shone with silvery gleam,
And in the moon's subduing beam
　　The signs of war
(Whose glory was my topmost dream)
　　Glittered afar.

XXI.

" Those were the times that tried men's souls ;"—
The blazing cannon's thunder rolls
Around the hills; no church bell tolls
   The soldier's fall ;
He passes to the goal of goals
   In crimson pall.

XXII.

My father and my elder brother
Their martial ardour could not smother,
So, bade adieu to home and mother,
   And rushed to battle ;
They fought, alas ! 'gainst one another,
   Like men of mettle.

XXIII.

In Carleton's ranks my father stood,
A loyal man of stubborn mood;
My brother—for his country's good—
   Led on by Green—
The routed foe with shouts pursued
   And weapons keen.

XXIV.

Pardon, dear folk, this slight digression,
Too grave to stamp a gay impression;
Old men forget themselves in session
    As journals tell ye:
But hearken now a full confession
    Of what befel me.

XXV.

I hurried on, 'twas wearing late,
With soft caresses in my pate;
I reached my charmer's cottage gate,
    But here I halted;
My grit, like some old pewter plate,
    Was tried—and melted.

XXVI.

I felt a weakness at the knee,
Large drops were running warm and free—
Like rillets hasting to the sea—
    Adown my cheeks,
I called on Heaven to pity me,—
    He finds who seeks.

XXVII.

My prayer was answered by a strain
Which fell, like magic on my pain ;
The songstress was my peerless Jane,
    Her voice I knew ;
The words on memory's leaves remain
    Like honey dew.

Song.

I

A little bird of plumage gay
  Sat singing in a myrtle tree ;
What think you did the birdie say ?
  What said it, love, to you and me?

2

It said be happy in the light
  Of love's young morn, when love is truth ;
Be happy ere has taken flight
  The witchery of dreaming youth.

3

An owlet sat at close of day
  Too-hoo-ing in a linden tree ;

What think you did the owlet say?
　What said it, love, to you and me?

4

It said, be wise ere comes the night
　Of lone repining, keep your truth,
Be wise and wed ere takes its flight
The witchery of dreaming youth.

XXVIII.

The song had ceased ; again I started,
So resolute, so joyous-hearted,
No earthly power could then have thwarted
　　My steps from Jane ;
A little laughing Cupid darted
　　From vein to vein.

XXIX.

Thus, marching forward to the door,
"O Jane, dear Jane," I muttered o'er,
"For thee, my love, I'd venture more
　　Than did Leander
In swimming to his Hero's shore
　　A fearless gander !"

XXX.

I gained the porch, one victory that,—
A moment paused, and lightly sat
My fashionable Sunday hat
    Upon three hairs;
I rapped, my heart went pit-a-pat,
    With all my airs.

XXXI.

I rapped, and heard a sweet "Come in,"
Don Quixote-like, I set my shin,
Resolved to dash through thick and thin
    Upon adventure:
Three inches higher I raised my chin
    And thus I enter.

XXXII.

We met, kind Venus! Oh! we met,
And how could I that hour forget?
Love's glorious summer sun is set
    With aged Peter,
But here its twilight lingers yet
    And warms his metre.

XXXIII.

" Pardon me, Bird of Night," said I,
" I heard you sing while passing by,
And such a voice as thine might vie
   With Orpheus' lyre,
Which charmed all things beneath the sky
   At his desire.

XXXIV.

Its melody, as authors write,
Stayed listening torrents in their flight,
And shook the mountains with delight,
   While round him came
Wild forest beasts (a wondrous sight!)
   Subdued and tame."

XXXV.

This precious gem of pagan lore,
I picked up somewhere weeks before,
And laid it up in secret store
   With shrewd design,
To bring it forth in this amour
   And make it shine.

XXXVI.

Her cheek, as fair as blow of peach,
Grew crimson at this flattering speech ;
She placed a chair within my reach
  And said : " Be seated,—
Where did you learn, bright youth, to preach
  Your brain is heated."

XXXVII.

This taunting stroke I ill could bear,
And answered only with a stare,
Then dropped like lead, into the chair,
  And down she sat,
First having, with a courteous air,
  Bestowed my hat.

XXXVIII.

Now snugly seated face to face,
Between us just three boards, a space
I might have crossed with half a pace,
  But modesty
Made wide, as any gulf, that place
  'Twixt bliss and me.

XXXIX.

"That song," said she " you heard me sing,
Is nothing but a foolish thing ;
My folk, the whole live-gathering,
    Are gone to-night,
And music seems to make Time's wing
    Move swift and bright."

XL.

" Now or never, do or die,
Here's a lucky chance," thought I,
" No bar to love, no gazer nigh
    Our bliss to damp ; "
While kindness streamed from Jane's bright eye
    As from a lamp.

XLI.

Her half-bared bosom rose and fell
Like placid ocean's gentle swell ;
Her glance like summer sunshine fell
    Upon my heart ;—
How could I else than act too well
    A lover's part ?

XLII.

" Then you are *solus*, dearest maid,"
She laughed outright, and blushing said,
" Have you commenced the *dearing* trade
So soon, fair lad ? "
This jeering banter, promptly paid,
'Most drove me mad.

XLIII.

Till then I deemed myself, a man,
And lord of every amorous plan,
Now through my limbs a shiver ran,—
The air grew chill;
" Your cheeks," said she " are thin and wan
Pray, are you ill ? "

XLIV.

I smothered down a heavy sigh,
And gayly made her this reply :—
" If I were ill would you deny
A cure for me ? "
" O, all I could," said she, " I'd try
To comfort thee."
17

XLV.

Such kind, endearing words as these
Brought me almost upon my knees :
" I've got " said I, " a sad disease
   Which you can cure,
And set my aching heart at ease,
   Of this—be sure."

XLVI.

A sudden change subdued her look,
The rosy blood her cheek forsook,
She rose,—her silken hood she took,
   And looking in it,
Said : " Please excuse me while I look
   Outside a minute."

XLVII.

A quiet respite now I got
To stare about the room and plot;
It was a neat though humble cot
   Of wooden frame ;
A home, it was devoted nct
   To folly's name.

XLVIII

Here stood the huge-rimmed spinning wheel,
There sat a tray of Indian meal,
And overhead, like polished steel,
  A musket lay ;
A dog and puss together reel
  In frantic play.

XLIX.

Thus peering round with random glance,
I saw, or thought I saw, by chance,
Three seeming deities advance,
  My soul alarming,
But soon they caused my feelings dance
  With speeches charming.

L.

The first began : " My name is Hope;
To give thy fancy brighter scope
I come,—no longer sit and mope
  With love concealed :
If thou thy bosom fully ope
  The Nymph will yield."

LI.

Then Cupid, neither blind nor lame,
With full-packed quiver smiling came;
I feared the Paphian archer's game,
       For well I knew
That all his darts were tipt with flame,
       And torture too.

LII.

"Ha! Ha!" quoth he, "my foolish boy,
If you with Hymen mean to toy,
I'll help him to some new employ."—
       From 'neath his wing
He drew his bow with look of joy,
       And twanged the string.

LIII.

Next Courage spoke: "Lo! youthful guest,
I've come to fire thy timid breast;
What Hope and Love have just addressed
       Must not prove vain;
This night thy soul must be confessed
       To lovely Jane.

LIV.

That maid for whom thou'st banged the head
Of Sleep so oft upon thy bed,
Until he groaning from thee fled,
            Is here alone :
Then ask her boldly will she wed
            And be thine own."

LV.

Pardon this wild Homeric flight,
And I will stoop from airy height ;
'Tis truth I came to tell to-night,
            And therefore ought
To paint my picture not too bright,
            As I've been taught.

LVI.

Those shades divine had passed from view
When, with no less celestial hue,
My earthly goddess, warm and true
            Returned, and then
I looked into her eyes of blue
            Again—again.

LVII.

"It is," said she, "a lovely night,
And though my folk are not in sight,
They soon will be, if all is right,
    For 'tis the hour."
Now was the time for Love to light
    On Fortune's flower.

LVIII.

Her fragrant breath my passion fanned,
I burned to kiss—or press her hand,
But feared to try—you understand,—
    Lest I should rue it,
Till Love upon a sudden planned
    How I might do it.

LIX.

I told her I had learned an art
Consoling to a maiden's heart:
"You've got," said I "a little chart
    Which I can read,
And from its dainty lines impart
    What you should heed.

LX.

Can tell how soon you'll be a bride,
How many beaux you have denied,
How many heirs you'll raise to pride
    Their native land:
All this, and more I can decide
    Within your hand."

LXI.

" Palmology your art they style,"
Replied the girl with sceptic smile,
" I know you think but to beguile
    My simple pate;
But there's my homely hand awhile,
    Now read my fate."

LXII.

I sprang enraptured from my seat
To grasp the prize, and play the cheat,
I seized it—Oh ! the electric heat
    That shook me now !
I heard our hearts like drumsticks beat
    Strange row-da-dow.

LXIII.

I lost my gay design of flattery,
My ravished eyes grew somewhat watery,
Her face was Love's galvanic battery,
    Her arms the poles,
So Peter's heart was blown to tatters, ye
    Pitying souls!

LXIV.

Close by the nymph I trembling stood,
And all her heaven of beauty viewed;
My lips to hers I rashly glued—
    But on the spot,
In this voluptuous attitude
    Poor Pete is caught!

LXV.

Back flies the door, the family all
Rush with a noise into the hall,
Led by a figure grim and tall,
    With whip in hand:
"You daring rogue," I heard him bawl,
    "What's this I find?"

LXVI.

As drops the fox the fluttering hen,
When dogs and boys and armed men
At once attack him in the pen,
    With furious din,
So I now dropped the blushing Jane,
    And hung my chin.

LXVII.

But, oh ! the man who bore the whip
Began to stamp, and swear, and rip,
And laid the lash upon my hip
    So cutting sore,
I gave a three-yard Yankee skip,
    And gained the door.

LXVIII.

Outside I got, but close behind
My foe pursued with speed of wind,
His sounding thong with crimson lined
    My smarting back,
And peeled from off my shanks the rind
    At every crack.

LXIX.

I roared, and yelled, and danced a-head,
Invoking powers of sacred dread,
Till by superior speed I fled
      His lash unkind :
But Oh ! my hat—must it be said ?—
      Was left behind !

LXX.

Homeward I drove, bare-headed, lame,
Smarting with love, and stripes, and shame—
Oh ! such a medley-mongrel-flame
      As this, ye fair !
Made Peter curse your sacred name,
      And bang the air.

LXXI.

I thought of drowning, poison, shooting.
My hopes, like routed ranks retreating,
Left me the crust of sorrow eating,
      Till dawn of day,
When sons of Mars their drums were beating
      Not far away.

LXXII.

I heard the clash of bayonets ring—
I ran—I flew on glory's wing
To serve my country, not my king,
      Nor served in vain;
Our deeds the future bards will sing
      In epic strain.

LXXIII.

To Jane Levay I bade adieu,
And ere to manhood's years I grew
The tidings o'er the country flew
      That Jane was married;
So overboard my hopes I threw,
      And single tarried.

LXXIV.

Now, when I draw my pension fee
I view it with an eye of glee,
And think: " My courtship, 'tis to thee
      I owe this guerdon:"
Then if I take a fortnight's spree,
      I beg your pardon.

LXXV.

My tale is told; and if my skill
Has charmed away one earthly ill,
Has made one aged bosom thrill,
  Let cynics frown,
The few who know my follies will
  Not-write them down.

LXXVI.

For you, my boys, with ardent eyes,
Whose nightly dreams and daily sighs
Are urged by beauty's maddening dyes
  And glossy curls,
Till older—mark me !—I advise,
  Keep from the girls.

FEAR OF BLINDNESS.

A horror, like the darkness of the tomb,
    Came over me when told,
That I might lose the brightness and the bloom,
    The blessed green and gold
Of landscapes, and the circuit of the skies.
    If doomed such ill to bear,—
If never more, indeed, these clouded eyes
    May taste their daily fare
Of books and beauty's charm, it were unwise
    To yield me to despair.

Twin guides, that from the dawn of life till late
    Your lamps for me have borne,
If weary of your task you hesitate
    To serve me further, worn

And vexed with slavish toil, demanding rest
    Myself alone I chide,
And grateful are the heavings of my breast,
    For light so long supplied
By two such faithful friends, abused, opprest,
    Your rights, poor eyes! denied.

My soul, if fails thy hope, with patient brow
    Accept the outer dusk,
And trust the inner light that serves thee now
    To pierce the silken husk
Of truths that do impart a quiet joy.
    The self-illumined mind
Is not dependent for its best employ
    On outward things, defined
To outward sense ;—let aught this lamp destroy,
    And I were truly blind.

UNKNOWN.

(On receiving the portrait of a young lady personally
unknown to the author.)

Image of one whose lips and eyes
    Have never moved me with their spell;
Whose greeting smiles, and farewell sighs,
    To happier hearts their meaning tell.

The echo of thy life, to me,
    Is but as music heard in dreams;
Or like a cloud beyond the sea,
    Or foreign flowers by foreign streams.

And yet I know—who may not know?
    That these twin windows of the soul
Have had their hours of overflow,
    Their share of gladness and of dole.

I know, for 'tis " the common lot,"
   That oft within this comely brow
Angelic hope, and loving thought,
   Have reared fair castles, crumbled now.

The stars that all alike behold,
   The air we breathe, the sun that cheers,
Unite, and evermore enfold,
   The generations of the years.

And hence it needs no clasp of hands,
   Nor vocal utterance, face to face,
To feel those sympathetic bands
   That unify the human race.

FLORAL ENVOY.

To F. B.

I.

This envoy of flowers,
  A deputy meet,
Your birthday, my friend,
  Is instructed to greet,
And my kindliest wishes
  To kindly repeat.—
      Interpret aright
      In friendship's white light
What the beautiful flowers
  Would say, could they speak.
The sensitive flowers,
  All voiceless and weak,—
Their meaning, involved
  In their bloom and their breath,
Despairing to utter,
  They haste to their death.

II.

The sweet-scented flowers
  Must droop and decay,
But not what their delicate
  Pantings would say.
The messenger fails,
  But the message survives—
An essence, a spirit,
  That throbs in the lives
Of atoms too subtile
  For kinship with clay.

III.

All kindly emotion,
  That passes the portal
Of a heart that is truthful,
  Is thenceforth immortal:
In its mute transmigration
  From age unto age,
In the love of the maid
  In the thought of the sage,
It blossoms afresh,
  It persists without end,

Joins lover to lover,
   Binds friend unto friend.
Then, seeing that flowers
   And words are but weak,
Take care that to-night,
You interpret aright
What the sensitive flowers
   Would say could they speak.

ON THE DEATH OF A VETERAN JOUR
NALIST.

Great faith was his, a broadened light that shed
    An unremittant halo on his way,
    Out-shining moon, and stars, and solar ray,
By which his steps through stormy years were led ;
And while his soul on heavenly manna fed,
    The well adjusted balance, work and pray,
    He steadfastly observed from day to day,
Assured that faith divorced from work is dead.
For man's behoof the Christian hero wrought,
    Consistent, fearless, aiming for the right,
    His silvered locks conspicuous in the fight,
Whose purpose was release of limb and thought
From all enslaving bonds ; kind heart and brave !
No rest for him, no rest but in the grave !

HEART-HUNGER.

Dost thou do well, dear idol of my heart !
 To thrall me in the meshes of thy charms,
 To fill my constant soul with soft alarms,
Then coyly thrust me from thy love apart ?
Pluck from my breast, O pluck the mystic dart !
 Yield—or I perish—to these folding arms !
Assuage the hunger of this sick desire
That wraps me like an aromatic fire !—
 O lull with thy ambrosial breath the swarms
Of wounded thoughts that issue from my brain
 And seek thy presence, seek thee day and night,
 And on thy brow, and eyes, and lips alight,
Extracting aye a honey that is pain !—
 O, save me with thy kisses, love, or kill me quite !

TO A YOUNG AUTHOR ON HIS BIRTHDAY.

Friend of my later years, whose thoughts are set
　　To noble ends, despising the pursuit
　　Of vices which the instinct of the brute,
Incorporate in man, contends for yet ;—
Who out of boyhood's slavery and fret
　　Could issue like a sword-blade from its sheath,
　　Resolved by high endeavor to bequeath
Some good that future times may not forget,—
　　Press on, thy better fortune leads the way,
And thine is still the sesame of youth,
To which the door of many a hidden truth
　　Shall open,—so I dare to prophesy,—
And ancient Error, stubborn and uncouth,
　　Shall own thy strength and rue thy natal day.

TO G. I. AT STRATFORD-ON-AVON.

The leaf you plucked from Shakespeare's garden plot,
   And sent me, my most estimable friend,
The voyage of the salt sea injured not.
Green as it grew upon its native spot,
   It nestled 'mid the kindly words you penned.
The poet's genius, free from flaw or blot,
   In which Melpomene found naught to mend,
   My fancy with this leaflet loves to blend ;
But, though with care I guard it all my days,
   In fret of time 'twill fade and fall away,
   Like hope, once fresh, will crumble to decay.
Not so our Dramatist's perennial bays ;
Not so the bloom and sunshine of his Plays,
   Rejoicing in their immortality.

MERCY.*

Ye silent statesmen, fully armed with power
 To save or slaughter, spare the captive's life !
 The wild fanatic of a hapless strife,
Still fresh in manhood's summer-scented flower ;
Whose sense of wrong, discretion did devour,
 And, breaking from his children and his wife,
Feared not the hazard of the fatal hour,
 The ineffectual struggle, ever rife
With death and dungeons when rebellion fails.
 O, let humanity for mercy plead !
Risk not the victor's vengeance on the scales
Of Justice, lest our grieved November gales
 Waft on to future years the ruthless deed,
 And keen remorse to cooler thoughts succeed.

* Written in reference to the impending execution of Lonis Riel,
when it was hoped by many that his life would be spared.

LOVE AND DEATH.

[Arranged from fragments of MS. found in the port.
manteau of a young traveller who died suddenly at a
wayside inn in Idaho, in the year 1850.]

When toward me bends the shade of death,
And friends deplore my waning breath,
Let woman, flushed with vernal charms,
Support me in her tender arms,
And kindly let her bosom swell
For one who loved her sex too well.

And when the solemn change has come,
Should sorrow hold my angel dumb,
And dim her eyes with humid veil,
And fix them on my features pale,
My spirit, raised on wing to go,
Will hover o'er her breast of snow,
And on her saddened lips impress

The seal of love's farewell caress,
Then, if a tear-drop chance to roll
Adown her cheek, my flying soul
Will snatch the gem,—for earth too bright,—
And bear it to the realms of light ;
Nor there the sparkling pledge resign,
But hoard it as a thing divine,
And smile to see its feeble ray
Blend with thy beams, Eternity !

And now, dear woman, gently press
Those lids that claim thy tenderness,
And hide those faded orbs of blue
That oft in rapture rolled on you,
And through the silent hours of night
Cradled your image in their light.
Now let thy loving fingers close
Those lips above their ivory rows,
And think, while you the task fulfil,
How oft thine own have made them thrill,
How oft, with youthful passion warm,
Their kisses told my heart's alarm,
Enough ; retire, forever blest ;
Let meaner hands perform the rest.

Next, let nor clown nor knave presume
To bear my relics to the tomb ;
Let bards and sages, men of mind,
Convey it thence with bosoms kind,
And think, along the solemn way,
" We bear a brother's weight to-day."
Let no grim priest of narrow view
My spirit's mystic flight pursue,
And o'er my corse his terrors sound
To awe his trembling dupes around,
And stupidly profane the end
Of slandered Truth's devoted friend.

Now place me in my rayless bed,
And carve these lines above my head :

" This simple mound conceals from sight,
A brother of poetic light.
His heart was Love's volcanic throne,
Love, the sole king he e'er would own.
All men, of every hue of skin,
He reckoned as his nearest kin ;
He looked where'er oppression trod,
And felt the inward flash of God,

And prayed with an immortal hope
For Freedom's universal scope.
Titles and power by outrage won,
And handed down from sire to son,
He ever held in utter scorn,
And honoured most the lowly born.
His follies, oh ! the vast amount—
Forgive them ere you stop to count,
And let oblivion's velvet pall,
In charity conceal them all.

" Inquirest thou the poet's creed ?
'Twas brief, but served his utmost need :
Truth is divine, wherever found,
On Christian or on pagan ground ;
Engraven on the hearts of men
Are God's commandments, more than ten ;
The universe his laws proclaim,
To learn them be my constant aim ;
Goodness and mercy, holy these
In Jesus or in Socrates ;
The glory of an earthly span
Is service to our fellow man.
'Twas thus with chastened heart he thought,

Nor cared what theologians taught ;
And if he erred to an excess
In not believing more, or less,
Ye who accuse, depart in fear,
And spare his bones your censure here.
If your own merits far excel
The poet's troubled life, 'tis well.
If in a truer light you live,
Go ! learn to pity and forgive."

THE END.